CRYSTAL CLEARING

Angel Jain

Book Vine Press
2516 Highland Dr.
Palatine, IL 60067

This book is dedicated to the belief
that one day, we all will live in a world
just like Crystal Clearing…

PROLOGUE
1971

A boy runs deep into a forest, while playing hide and seek with his friends. He realizes that he has run too deep. He starts to panic. The elders in his village say to never go this deep into the forest, for fears of the wolves that stalk the forest floor. He feels as if someone or something is watching him as he moves swiftly through the forest floor, littered with leaves and twigs. He knows that he should turn and get out of the quiet, yet dangerous woods, but something catches his eyes. A glittering gold colour shines from a distance. Curious, he goes closer and sees a golden plaque laying under a tree. It has 4 small squares each with a small symbol. A cat, a person, a cloud, and a heart. He reached out to try and touch it, but just then, the plaque shined even brighter. It was almost brighter than sunlight. He thought that the ground was starting to shake. The boy turned and ran as fast as he could. "Mama! Papa!" He shouted…

PART ONE

A camping trip gone wrong

Holly Mitchell ran to the living room, dropping her school bag along the side of the front door. She settled on the couch and turned on the tv. "Yes!" she says, happily. "Spring break is finally here! That means I get to stay home and watch all the episodes of "The King of Lights.""

Just before the show started, Holly's phone rang. "Hey Latisha, what's up?" She asked, pulling her legs up. "Holly!! You will never believe what happened. My parents just told me that I'm going to a Soccer Camp over the break. I have no idea why they would need to send me to camp this year. But I have to go. I'm SOOO sad I can't be home for our King of Lights marathon." Holly frowned. "Aw man! Hey at least you're going to a soccer camp, you love soccer, don't you?" She was trying to make Latisha feel better. "Yeah, but what do I like better? King of lights. You know that Holly." she sighed. "Oh well, at least I can watch the first episode." The sound of a muffled rummaging came from the other end. Then came Latisha's sad voice, which was usually so cheery. "Hey, um I gotta go, talk to you soon, I guess. Actually, I don't know if they allow phones at camp. But um, Bye." Holly sighed, obviously disappointed at the news. But she tried to look on the bright side. At least she wasn't going to camp. So, when Latisha came back, Holly could tell her all that had happened. That's what a good friend would do.

The sound of sci-fi music jerked Holly from her daydream. "Yes!!" She cheered, leaning forward eagerly. Just when the beginning credits were done. The Tv screen turned blank. "What?!" She cried. The ugly laugh from her little brother

Hendrick and her parents' cheerful chirping gave her the answer. They had just come home from work and school. "Hello, little cream cake. How was the last day of school before spring break???" Her mom sang, putting a brochure on the table. Oddly, Hendrick was holding another brochure too. "Oh! Hi mom. It was great!!!" Holly replied through clenched teeth. "But, um I was kind of starting to watch the King of Lights, so, you know if you don't mind turning the tv back on, that would be awesome." Holly's father came and stood next to her mom. "Oh, you don't want to watch that alien movie, honey. We have a better surprise for you." He said, grinning. Holly tried to remain as calm as she could. "Dad, King of Lights isn't an alien movie. It's about a bunch of kids who get lost on a strange planet and discover this whole new kingdom of humans where they meet the king of lights. And the best part…" "Oh, Holly aren't you too old to be watching these kids' movies? I mean, you're 14 years old. A couple of months later, you're going to be 15." Her mother asked, arms crossed. "Mom! King of Lights is rated 13+. And it's educational. Well, I mean some parts are. Like for example, did you know that there is a planet made of diamonds that's twice the size of Earth? It's most likely covered in diamonds and graphite. And where did I learn that from? The King of Lights." Holly looked at her parents, to see their reaction. They both looked unimpressed. Really unimpressed. "Well Holly, we'll talk about this later. But first, don't you want to know what the surprise is?" "Gees, I wonder what could be better than King of Lights." Holly rolled her eyes, as she followed her parents to the side table.

Her eyes fell on the brochure. Hendrick followed suit, with an ugly smirk on his face. "We already talked to Hendrick about this in the car." Mom said, nodding towards Holly's little brother. "So, your father and I found out that we have an important company meeting next week for two days. But it's out of town. And we didn't want to leave you two here alone. So…" Holly's eyes widened. "So? So, what?" she asked impatiently. She did not have a good feeling about where this conversation was going.

"So." Her father started. "Our co-worker gave us these brochures." he picked up the blue paper. "They are for a nature camp that runs for 10 days time." Holly froze. This could only mean one thing. "So, you're telling me that you signed me up for this nature camp?" she asked, carefully. Her mother nodded. "Of course, we did! Just look at this place." Dad opened the pamphlet. "Hikes, nature walks, Nature education, 3 square meals a day. And the cost was incredibly cheap. What more could you ask for?" Holly felt like she had been punched in the stomach. "Nooo!" She cried. She wanted to scream even louder. "Holly! What's the matter?" Her mother asked, coming near her. "The matter is you signed me up for something I never wanted to do. You know I would rather watch a sci fi movie than go to nature camp." "Oh, Holly, stop with your sci fi lecture. I heard enough of that already. You need to get out more, and not stay cooped up inside." Holly couldn't believe this! "Me? What about Hendrick? At least I play soccer, all I ever see him do is play video games." Mom sighed. "Holly, Hendrick is a child, you—" "He's ten." Holly snorted. "Ok, Holly that's enough. You're going and that is final." Dad interrupted, sternly. "uhg!" she screamed as she raced upstairs to her room.

Holly couldn't believe it! Her parents had signed her up for camp. Now, she could never tell Latisha what happened in the movie because Holly herself was going to camp. And that wasn't even the worst part! What type of camp was she going to? A nature camp! If it had been sports camp, she wouldn't have been this mad. Even though going to camp wasn't exactly the best, at least she could enjoy the sports. But Nature camp? Come on, what could be so interesting about going on hikes and nature walks?

After a few moments of laying on her bed venting her frustration out, and a long ranting session with Latisha, (who was obviously very disappointed at the news) Holly decided that she was just going to have to deal with it and stop laying around feeling sorry for herself. She changed from her hoodie and cargo pants into denim shorts and a white tank top. Then she grabbed her laptop and started researching this nature camp. But there were hundreds of nature camps and Holly had forgotten the name of this particular camp. Well, she was just going to have to go through them all. So, she started her search.

A few minutes in, her parents came knocking on the door and tried explaining to her why they thought this was a nice idea and that they didn't mean to make her feel bad. Of course Holly knew that, so she said it was fine and that she could handle it. Everyone was okay so her parents left, and she continued researching. Finally, Holly found the camp website. "Green Vine Camp." She read, scrolling through the site. "A fun and educational camping experience for the cheap cost of $250 For 10 days." Great! She'd be staying there for 10 days. By then, "The King Of Lights" would be finished!

The reviews from other people seemed ok. But then, one caught her eye. It said, "Green Vine Camp is nice and educational, but just pray that your kids aren't stuck with Pam, one of the councillors. She is super careless and is sometimes grouchy and cranky. If your child is in her group, then good luck. Trust me you need it." Holly couldn't help but laugh a little. So, if she was not stuck with Pam, things wouldn't be too bad. But then she had a second thought. It had said that she was careless, so that would mean she could probably get away with a few little sneaky phone calls and scroll throughs. A small smile slipped onto her lips. Just then, her mom called her down for dinner. Wow! She had spent longer than she imagined researching Camp Green Vine.

Dinner was pretty easy going. Her mom and dad were apologizing and explaining to her again. After Holly said it was fine again, they started talking about the meeting that they were going to. They talked about how excited they were and babbled on about this and that. But all that time, Holly was thinking about Green Vine Camp. For some weird reason a dark, creepy feeling rose inside of her. She shook it off, of course. After all, she had delicious, juicy steak to finish off…

On Saturday, Holly spent the day with Latisha, who would be leaving for camp tomorrow. At that moment, she was helping Latisha with packing up. "Can you believe that we're both going to camp?" she pouted, taking some pants out of her closet. Holly sighed. "Latisha, you're luckier than me. At least you're going to a sports camp. I'm going to a nature camp! Can you imagine me going on hikes and nature walks?" Latisha flipped her purple streaked hair over her shoulder. "Well, yeah that's true. Honestly Holly, that makes me feel so much better." Holly frowned. "Come on dude, don't make me feel worse than I already am."

Latisha was now stuffing everything into a blue suitcase. "Oof! Holly, I need help closing this thing!" Holly got up from Latisha's bed and helped her friend close the suitcase. "Really Lati? You're only going there for a week, do you really need this much clothes? I mean it's not like you're going on a month-long trip to Hawaii or anything." Latisha's eyes lit up. "Oh, I almost forgot to pack my new floral cleats! Thanks for the reminder!" Holly just shook her head. One thing was for sure. When she was at camp, she was going to miss Latisha's girly yet sporty personality…

On Sunday, it was Holly's turn to pack. She didn't need a suitcase though, just a duffel bag, packed with some tops and bottoms, a few snacks, a water bottle, a notebook and pen, a couple of toiletries, and her phone. She really wanted to bring her laptop, but there wasn't any space. Holly had learned that Hendrick and her wouldn't be going to the same camp, due to vacancy issues. It was still a nature camp, but just a different one. Holly was definitely relieved about this. At least she wouldn't have to deal with her annoying little brother. Now all she had to do was pick out a first day outfit. After a while of searching, she settled on black denim overalls and a white T-shirt. Along with clothes, she also chose white sneakers and her favourite baseball cap. With everything ready, she had half the day left.

As she sat there wondering what to do, her cell phone rang. It was Latisha! Happier than ever, Holly answered straight away. "Omg I never thought I would hear your voice again for a whole week!!" Holly cried, gladly. "So, is camp horrible? Are they teaching you brutally?" She realized that she hadn't even let her friend talk. "Latisha?" "Um Holly, don't kill me for saying this, but I'm actually enjoying camp. I really like it here! We get lots of sport training, three delicious yet healthy meals and super fun activities. Plus, we all get a big cabin with our very own rooms and bathrooms. You don't really need to share it with anyone. Honestly, I'm enjoying myself here." Holly frowned. She couldn't help but feel a little jealous. "You know, I sometimes forget you're in a sports camp. And not nature camp. Like I will be, tomorrow." She said, playing with a loose string on her denim shorts. "Holly I'm sorry, but maybe you should try and think that camp is going to be fun. I mean yeah, I know it's nature camp but that can have its perks, Holly. Take me for example, I was so not looking forward to going to camp. But look at me now! I'm seriously enjoying this. And it's only been a day!" Holly wanted to tell her that sports camp and nature camp were different things, but she knew that Latisha was just trying to help her out. So, she pretended to be cheered up. "Thanks Lati. You're a good friend." "No prob! Hey I gotta go, they're serving meat lasagna for lunch! TTYL Holly!" And that was it. Probably the last phone call she could make to Latisha for about a week…

The next day, Holly woke to the sound of her phone alarm ringing. "Huh?" she said, startled. She didn't remember setting up her alarm. And definitely not this early. It was only 6:00! Holly groaned. Her parents probably set it up while she was fast asleep. "Goood morning Holly! Come on lazy head wake up. Do you know what day it is today? It's camp daaaaayyy!" Her mom sang, pulling the blankets away. "uhg, mom can I have a few more minutes?" she asked pulling the blankets up. "Nope! You need to get ready early so that we can be at camp right on time. It's not good to be late on the first day. And besides your father is making crepes. Your favourite!" her mom chirped, walking to the door. Holly groaned again. She didn't sleep well at all last night. Tossing, turning, weird dreams…it was all so strange because Holly was the type of person to sleep straight away when her head hit the pillow. But she shook it all away and reluctantly got up.

Sure enough, when she came downstairs, a delicious crepe was waiting for her on the table. "Good morning, Holly." her father called from the kitchen. "Morning dad!" she called, walking to her seat. Her mom was there with a half-eaten crepe on her plate. She was busy looking at her laptop. Hendrick walked in rubbing his eyes. Holly snorted. "Wow, I can't believe you actually woke up this early, Hendrick." Her little brother glared. "Hmp! Says the girl who never wakes up on time on school days." He shot back. "Holly, Hendrick that's enough. I don't need you two bickering first thing in the morning. Now finish your crepes and go get ready." Mom said, without looking up from her laptop. They did as she said. Holly took a big bite out of her crepe. The scrumptious chocolate drizzle and berries inside made her realize that this was probably the last tasty meal she was going to have in a week. So, Holly decided to enjoy every single bite…

After brushing her teeth and changing into her black denim overalls and t shirt, she brushed her short blonde hair and tied it into a ponytail.

Then came putting on her sneakers and baseball cap and she was all ready. With her duffel bag hung on her shoulder, and a deep breath, Holly shut her bedroom door and started down the stairs. Along the way she saw her brother coming out of his room with an extremely disappointed sigh. Holly wondered what happened to him.

Her parents were already waiting in the minivan, buzzing about the business trip. Holly climbed into the backseat. "All ready, Holly?" her dad asked. Holding up her duffel bag, she answered, "Yup, everything's in here." Mom smiled, approvingly. "Love this look, Holls. Seems like you want to make a good first impression." Holly smirked. After Hendrick climbed in beside her, they were all set to get going.

For most of the car ride, Holly looked out the window, watching people walking their pets, and kids running around. It was a beautiful day in Cobblestone Valley. She saw some of the kids from her middle school walking about, enjoying this gorgeous day and enjoying the first day of spring break, not having to worry about going to camp.

But a while into the ride, Holly noticed Hendrick sitting quietly beside her, looking down at his shoes. Strange! She thought. Hendrick was never this quiet. She placed a hand on his knee and asked, "You ok?" Hendrick looked up and shrugged. His face was almost sad. Holly's big sister vibes said something was horribly wrong. Sure, he was an annoying little worm sometimes, but that didn't mean Holly liked seeing her brother look so down and unhappy. She bit her lip, considering something. Finally, after a sigh, she took off her baseball cap, her favourite one to exact, and held it. From the corner of her eye, she could see Hendrick watching curiously. With a final, silent goodbye, Holly reached and placed it on Hendrick's head. Startled, he started pulling it off, but Holly stopped him. "No, keep it. Consider it as, um you know, a going-to-camp present." She tried. Holly thought he was going to laugh his signature ugly laugh, like he usually did, but was surprised to see a genuine smile on Hendrick's face. He turned back to the window, a hand still on his cap and a smile still on his face. Holly sighed, relieved. She had no idea it would be this easy. With a smile and knowing that Hendrick was ok, she drifted into a nap…

A nudging woke Holly up from a long nap. She rubbed her eyes and saw Hendrick, still with her cap on, patting her on the shoulder. "Hendrick, what's up? she asked, yawning. "we're here." Holly frowned. "Here where? I thought we—" she didn't need to continue. Through the window, she saw a circular sign, held up by tree branches on either side, that read "Green Vine Camp." A few kids and their parents were waiting by the sign. Holly gulped. For some pathetic reason, she felt nervous and scared. "Holly, sweetheart, we're here." mom was saying. Despite her unwanted worry, she slowly got out of the car. Everyone else came out, also, probably to say their goodbyes. Her mom embraced her first. "Be good Ok? And listen to the councillors. And don't forget your—" "yeah I know mom, you don't have to worry so much about me." Holly assured her. Dad was up next, giving her a pat and quick hug. "Have fun, Holly." He said, with a smile. Hendrick was last, and while their parents were walking away to the car, he took the opportunity to surprise Holly by giving her a big hug. "Woah! Dude you're gonna crush me at this rate!" she wiggled out of Hendrick's embrace but was genuinely touched. "I'm going to miss fighting with you when I get to camp." He said, finally letting go of his sister. "Are you kidding?!

That's the part I'm going to miss the most too!" Holly said smiling. Hendrick smirked. "Really though? Even more than your King Of Lights show?" Holly rolled her eyes and shook her head, as Hendrick ran to the car, only turning to wave and smirk. As the car pulled out to the road, Holly once again waved to everyone.

With a deep breath she turned and stood behind some kids, wondering what to do. The kids seemed to just be standing there, some looking at their phones, others looking around anxiously. After a couple minutes, four adults, all in matching brown uniforms, walked up from the forest. There were two men and two ladies. A girl with dark skin and curly brown hair stepped forward and began speaking, "hello everyone! Welcome to Green Vine Camp. We're all so glad that you signed up for nature camp. My name is Tammy and I'm the lead camp councillor." Tammy gestured towards a dark skinned man. "Hey guys, I'm Tim and I help out mostly with making the food. You guys are going to love the meals here!" He said. *Yeah we'll see about that.* Holly murmured to herself. Next up, was a boy about 18 or 19. "Hey dudes and dudettes, I'm Jeff, another one of the camp councillors. Just side note, this is my first year volunteering at camp so, please bear with me" A few kids giggled. Lastly came a tall, pretty girl with an athletic build and blonde ponytail. "Hey guys, I'm Linda, and yeah, you guessed it, I'm another councillor. I'm mostly in charge of organizing the super fun activities you get to do, like hikes, nature walks, games just to mention a few." Linda smiled. Holly liked her. She was fierce and strong, but with just the right amount of humour.

The leader, Tammy, looked around and motioned for someone to come. The footsteps coming from the forest were loud. Holly gulped. At sleepovers, she and Latisha would always theorize big giant monsters and fantasy creatures, like the ones in "The King Of Lights" roaming around all the bushy forests in Cobblestone Valley. But Holly never expected them to actually exist! The footsteps grew near and Holly braced herself for the worst. *It's coming!* she thought, holding her duffel bag closer. It's *almost here*! *Getting closer and closer and…here it is, the monstrous beast…with a baseball cap? And a brown uniform that says… Camp Green Vine?*—Holly shook her head, relieved and faintly disappointed.

Holly took a glance at this councillor. A big woman, with short red hair and bangs. One look, and Holly recognized her immediately. No need for second thoughts. A name flashed in her head like a lightbulb. *Pam!* The councillor took a giant step forward. She had a small, pinched face and Holly noticed how frosty her bright hazel eyes were. "Alright, hello kids. I'm the last councillor here and my name is Pam." She said in a nasally voice and a slightly unhappy tone. Holly smiled, triumphantly. She was right! Tammy, the camp leader, stepped forward. "Alright campers, just clarifying, this is a 10 day program that goes from today, Monday, till next Wednesday. You'll be leaving Wednesday afternoon. Like Linda mentioned earlier, You'll be doing hikes, nature walks and a whole bunch of other fun stuff. We're sure you guys are going to love all the exciting activities we have planned for you!" She looked over at Tim, who grinned. "Now comes the yummy part…the food! We have a lot of savoury dishes that we are planning to make. Remember, if you don't like something, take small amounts. Do not waste anything!" "And also, if you have any food allergies, report it straight away to your assigned councillor." Tammy piped in. "Speaking of assigned councillor, you will all be divided into groups of about 7 or 9 and your assigned councillor will be one of us. We are going to be the leaders of your groups to explain the activities and just help you out. Each group will be appointed to a different chore. Tim's group will be in charge of making the food. Jeff's group will help with serving and washing. Linda's team will be in charge of setting up games and activities, my team will be on cleaning duty and lastly, Pam's group will be on cabin clean up. We will try to rotate every 2 days, so everyone gets a chance at doing everything."

Tammy turned to Linda, who handed her a clipboard. "Ok without further ado, let's put you all into your groups." She called out a couple of names and asked them to step forward. "Alright you guys are group 1, Tim's team. Please follow him to your cabins and he will tell you what to do." Next was Jeff's team, followed by Linda's. A handful of kids were left over. Tammy called a couple more names. Holly's name wasn't in there. It was either Tammy or Pam. Holly held her breath. "Alright, you guys are my group!" Tammy smiled energetically. "Kids left over, yup you guessed it, you all are on Pam's team!"

Tammy gestured towards her group of kids. Pam rolled her eyes and pulled out a small notebook from her uniform pocket. She sniffed and started talking. "Well, if it wasn't clear already, you're my batch of kids. And if you forgot already, I'm Pam. Now follow me to your cabins. Once we're there, we'll go over some basic rules and take attendance. After that, we will be giving you one hour of free time to do, I don't know, whatever you kids want to do. Then at 12:00, we will be coming back here." She sighed heavily and looked as if she would much rather be cleaning up a pigsty than being here. She reached towards her fanny pack. "Just gimme a moment first." She said while rummaging around in her pack.

Holly set her duffel bag down and crossed her arms. She looked towards the forest, which seemed to be calling her to walk in. Holly shook her head. She slowly turned around expecting to see nothing in particular, but that was where she was wrong. Holly gasped, speechless. Right there standing in front of her was… HIM!! Chestnut brown hair, crystal blue eyes, devious yet absolutely cute grin. There he was bright as day. Logan Fitzgerald!

Holly couldn't believe her eyes! Logan though, seemed to take no notice of her surprise. "Hey, Holly Mitchell! Long time no see, dude!" Immediately, she took her duffel bag, turned the other way, and started walking towards the front where most of the other kids where. By now, Pam had zipped her Fanny pack and was motioning them to follow her. Holly tried to speed up, but Logan was just too quick. "Woah, Holly slow down. Are you preparing for a speed walk competition or something? Cause if you are, then there's definitely a chance of you getting first place." Holly closed her eyes. *No this can't possibly be happening! Spending 10 days in nature camp? Bad, but bearable. Spending 10 days in nature camp with him?! Unbearable!!* "Come on Mitchell, talk to me! I never remember you being the quiet kid." Holly clenched her teeth. "For goodness sake Logan, what do you want?" By now, the group had walked into a small space with two big white cabins, one labeled, "group 5 Cabin 1" and another saying "Cabin 2" Pam took the memo pad and started going over some basic rules and what was tolerable and what was not. But for Holly, all she heard was, blah blah blah, because her mind wandered to fourth grade, where she first met Logan. She could remember so clearly…

It was the first day of fourth grade, and since Latisha was in another class, and Holly wasn't really best friends with anyone else, she was worried who she would hang out with for the next year. As she was walking down the halls, she bumped into a boy. "Oh I'm so sorry!" The boy says, turning as bright as a tomato. "That's ok. I'm sorry too." She had said. She peered at him. "Hey, are you new here? I've never seen you before." The boy shyly nodded. "I'm Logan Fitzgerald. I moved here from Shilo Hill." She extended out a hand. He shook it, happily. "Holly Mitchell. Nice to meet you. Who's your teacher?" The boy fidgeted with his jacket zipper. "Umm, I have Ms. Garner, but umm, I don't know where her classroom is." Logan looked down at the floor, reddening. Holly grinned. "Don't worry! I'm in Ms. Garner's class, too. I've been to this school since kindergarten, so I know where the class is. Come on, follow me!" She grabbed Logan's hand and pulled him to Ms. Garner's class. After that day, Holly and Logan bonded over their liking of sports, and became best friends! With Latisha, the three became inseparable. Two years passed and it was in middle school that things started to change.

First year, sixth grade to be exact, was fine. A week or so had passed, and Holly, Logan and Latisha were gathered in a little corner of the cafeteria. "So, what clubs or teams are you guys thinking of joining?" Holly had asked them. Logan pulled out three small green forms. "I picked these up from the office, on my way here from Math class. Basically there is a list of clubs and sports teams, each with a small description, and a checkbox. All you have to do, is check off which ones you want to join and fill in a bit of info and then that's it! You're done!" He grinned. "Sick!" Latisha says, grabbing a form. "For sports, I think I'm only going to join soccer. Cause the rest, just ain't my things. And also Holly, you better join in with me." Latisha warned, jokingly. "Because I checked it off in pen and there is no way I can erase." Logan smirked. "I have white out. You know, if you wanted to…" Latisha hit him in the head with her lunch bag, playfully. "Ok, you guys can choose from all the different sports teams you want, just know I'm only going to join soccer." She peered at the paper. "I see some really awesome clubs here so I was thinking of joining some of those. But you do you!" She smiled, examining the paper. Logan turned to Holly, with a disappointed face. "Hey! There's no football. No fair." He crossed his arms. "My brother's a senior in high school and they have football! So why can't we?" He pouted. Holly giggled. "Logan just imagine 11 or 12 year olds in big football uniforms crashing into each other!" Logan rolled his eyes and flexed his arm. "Yeah, but look at me! I have more muscle than my older brother. And he's a high school senior." He joked. Holly took a look at the sheet. "Hey, look Logan! There's basketball here! You looove basketball just as much as you like football." Logan immediately perked up. "Basketball? Nice." Logan eagerly checked it off. Holly sighed. "I wish I could join with you, but basketball is the only sport I absolutely fail in. Probably because I'm short." Logan let out a laugh. "Yeah, I'm sorry I can't join soccer, too. My footwork is terrible. My strength is all in my arms." He skimmed through the form. "You know, since we aren't going to be on each other's teams why don't we pick one sport that we both can do? So we will have at least one sport that we can do together?" Holly grinned enthusiastically. "Awesome! Ok, on the count of three, yell out your second favourite sport! One, two, three…" "tennis!" They yelled in unison.

Just like that, Holly and Logan were absolute friends. That is until the sports started. The first soccer and basketball game against another school was happening on the same day. And because of Holly and Logan's super sport skills, They both led their teams into victory. It was like this for a while, even at the school championships, they won first place. Ever since then, Holly and Logan were super popular. Everyone knew them as "the sports twins" and they couldn't be happier. The whole year was like this. But when seventh grade came along and more victories behind it, the attention turned more to Logan, after he shot a hoop from across the court. Holly wasn't really all that jealous, but was tired of people inviting her friend to eat with them and giving him way too many high fives. But then he started avoiding her. Like really avoiding. He would always go to his friends on the team instead of her. Other than the occasional greetings, he didn't hang out with her anymore. Holly had cried in the washroom once, taken aback by this new changed Logan. She then made a decision. If Logan didn't want to hang out with her, then neither did she. Although it hurt, she wasn't going to let a person ruin her life. Latisha was still loyal to Holly, but sometimes, told her to go talk to him, and see what really happened. She would say, "I mean you guys were huge friends and honestly I don't think a little popularity would set you two apart like this.

Maybe you guys should talk it out." Even though she wanted to believe Latisha desperately, Holly strongly refused. She has never talked to him since. Although he sometimes tries to talk to her with his little joker attitude, she wouldn't talk back for more than a few seconds. Holly had never been so hurt in her life! But with Latisha by her side, crepes to comfort her and soccer to make her life fun, she was dealing well with a wound that would never really heal.

"Holly? Holly Mitchell?" Holly woke from her daydream as she felt a nudge on her arm. Logan pointed at Pam, with a bigger clipboard in her hands and looking around the group of kids. "Uhh here! I'm here!" Holly said quickly waving her hands. Pam looked Holly up and down and checked her name off the list. "Wow, Mitchell you really zoned out for a second there. Well, really not a second actually, for almost 10 minutes or so. Did you hear a word Pam was saying?" Logan asked. "Of course I did!" Holly lied. Logan smirked. "Oh Holly, you've never been good at lying." Holly glared at him. "Well, well, what's it to you?" Logan held up his palms. "Oh it's nothing to me. I'm just stating the facts." Holly was about to come up with a smart response, when Pam interrupted saying, "Alright kids, it's nearly 11 so it's time for your free time. Remember, we're going back to the entrance at 12. Now, for cabins, cabin 1 is for the girls, and cabin 2 is for the guys. Don't go peeking into each other's cabins, alright? Anyways there are five beds. You all have to decide who sleeps where and all that junk. So yeah whatever, off you go." Pam said, waving her hands. Holly sighed in relief. With the groups divided, there wasn't much chance of seeing Logan again. At least for the next hour. "Well Logan, have a very happy time at your cabin!" Holly said with fake cheer, as she rushed away, not waiting for a response from Logan.

Inside the cabin, there where 3 small beds lined up and a bunk bed further to the wall. Along with that there was a door at the side which was probably the bathroom. "We call dibs on the bunk bed!" Yelled two girls, who Holly assumed were bffs. Another girl, with a cool haircut, quickly walked to the single bed beside it. "Awe, man I really wanted the bunk bed!" Said the fourth girl, who had curly reddish-brown hair and thick black glasses. Shrugging, she took her luggage and went to one of the remaining beds. Holly followed behind. The bed was surprisingly comfortable. She put her duffel bag underneath and sat on her bed watching the other girls. The two bffs sat on the top bunker chatting deeply. Haircut girl had her headphones on and was scrolling through her phone. Curly hair was reading a comic, with a pile of books by her side. Holly wondered what to do herself. She hadn't really thought to bring her comics so her phone was the only option. Suddenly an idea popped into her head. *Latisha!* She quickly dialled Latisha's number, and was greeted by her cheerful voice. "Holly! Omg hi! How are you doing? How's camp? Oh gosh I have so much to tell you." Holly smiled, and leaned onto her fluffy pillow…

After a lengthy phone call with Latisha, and her saying that she should totally have a chat with Logan, Holly left her parents a text and scrolled through her phone, also writing a small journal entry in the notebook she had brought. Before she knew it, free time was over. They met back with the other kids and it was chore time. So, Holly cleaned the cabins with her other group mates.

Next came lunch, which consisted of some surprisingly good meatloaf and salad.(Tim was really not kidding when he said they were all going to love the food!)

Then it was time for a nature walk. Tammy gave them some tips to keep safe and off they went, into the beautiful, green forest. When they came back there was a bit more free time, since it was the first day, and Holly took the time to write another journal entry.

Dinner was sloppy joes (again, delicious!) and then there was fun campfire storytelling hour, where people volunteered to tell spooky stories. Holly loved that part of the day the most! Then, bedtime rolled around, and after brushing and changing into her pjs she climbed onto her bed and pulled the blankets all the way up. *Huh. This wasn't actually as bad as I thought it would be. I mean except for Logan sneaking up on me a couple times. But other than that, it was pretty fine, especially campfire storytelling hour.* Holly thought, satisfied. And in no time at all, she was fast asleep, ready to face whatever was going to happen tomorrow...

Tuesday and Wednesday were regular days. On Tuesday, after chores and lunch (delicious!),

Tammy spent the whole evening teaching the group how to identify plants and trees as well as teaching them some more hiking tips and "survival" tips. The day ended with dinner and campfire story hour.

Wednesday was similar, but this time the group went on an actual hike(Long, but totally worth it!). At the end of the trail, there was a zip line, going from one side of the mountain like hill to the other. Underneath was a clear blue river. Everyone got a chance to go across the zip line, after a demo from Linda. Holly was super excited! She had always wanted to try extreme sports! When it was her turn, Tammy had set her in place and she zoomed across, feeling a gust of cold wind in her hair. It was a good thing she tied her hair up. Linda was on the other side and unbuckled her as soon as Holly landed. "Great job, kiddo! You're definitely a brave girl. Not a hint of fear on your face, just pure enjoyment!" Linda gave her a high five. That made Holly day!

All in all, the days so far at camp, weren't that bad. Other than Logan talking to her, with fake sweetness, the last three days were pretty great!

On Thursday, as Holly was heading to breakfast, she noticed that Tammy, Linda, Jeff, Tim and Pam, were all huddled around, with big hiking backpacks on their backs. Holly got her food, and went to a table with comic book girl and haircut girl.

As she started digging in, Tammy clapped to get everyone's attention. "Good morning campers! Today, we have a surprise for you!" She announced. "Today we're going camping! Like, real camping, in the forest! We will be starting the hike this morning, and we will get to our destination in the afternoon or maybe at around 1 or 2pm, depending on how we go." Linda stepped forward. "If you were paying close attention to the lesson on Tuesday, you're all good to go! But those who weren't…" Linda smirked. Jeff cupped his hands around his mouth, and whispered, "good luck!" Kids giggled. Tammy grinned. "Exactly! Now eat fast, we leave at 9:00. And remember, bring all of the things you brought from home. Backpacks and duffel bags are fine, but if you brought a suitcase or luggage, come to us and we'll give you some hiking backpacks." Holly smiled as she dug into her omelette and bacon sandwich. Camping sounded like fun! She couldn't wait!

Holly dragged her duffel bag to where the other kids were waiting with Jeff and Pam. "Hello hello, Mitchell. How's life, so far? Are you excited to go camping?" Logan had sneaked up on her again. Holly groaned. "uhh…yeah totally." Logan nodded, and silently stared into the forest. *Strange! This is the first time he's actually been quiet when he's with me. Strange but fine.* Holly coughed, immediately breaking his daydream. "Uhh, so, how's—how's Charlie doing?" She asked, trying to sound nonchalant. "Huh? Ohh, Charlie! Yeah he's doing fine. Great actually. He's in his first year of medical school. Isn't that great?" Logan said, a twinkle in his eyes. Holly jerked up. "Wow really? That's awesome!" She said genuinely happy. "Uhh, I mean how nice." Holly brushed off some dust from her outfit, consisting of a red plaid button down and black jeans, with black high top sneakers. "So, what kind of doctor is he studying to be?" Logan beamed. "A paediatrician. He loves working with little kids, so this is perfect for him!" Holly remembered Charlie, Logan's elder brother, being so nice to her, when she first met him in fourth grade. He would make a perfect paediatrician!

Holly was about to ask Logan something, when Tammy's voice boomed up front. "Ok campers, since we have a big group here, we're going to split up. My group and Tim's group, are going to be together. Linda and Jeff, you guys are together. And Pam's group, you guys are going by yourself, but rest assured, you have the most number of kids in your group, so you should be fine. Now we're all going to take different trails to the same place, and see who's group can get there the fastest. The winning team will get a prize! Good luck!" She motioned for her and Tim's group to follow. Linda and Jeff lead their team towards the left of the forest. "Alright, follow me! And remember don't go off the trail! Only follow where I go!" Pam said in her nasally voice. Holly was at the back of the line. Logan had moved more to the front. Holly took her time, enjoying the green scenery. It was beautiful!

Just then from the corner of her eyes, she saw a large butterfly, with wings as clear as glass, with small star like patterns on it. Holly had never seen anything like it before. Curious, she slowly walked towards it, following in the direction it was headed. But, then it flew with extreme speed. Holly tried to keep up by running, but it was too fast. She stopped at a clearing of tall trees, unable to see the butterfly again. "Oh well, I'll just search it up on my phone." She shrugged and turned around, but then realized that she had ran way too far into the forest, and had lost sight of her group! "No! This can't be happening!" She shouted, backing away from the trees. "No, no, no, please tell me I'm dreaming, that I'm still in bed." She prayed. She looked around trying to find something that she had walked past, but nothing rang in her head.

Then she heard twigs crunching. Someone was near! She gasped. She slowly backed up, panicked. As she kept backing up, she didn't see where she was going, and bumped into something! Or someone! Without thinking, Holly turned around, and smacked it in the face. Hard. Only then, she realized, followed by the groan, that it was Logan! *Oh, what have I done?!* "Logan! Oh, my goodness, I am so sorry!" Holly exclaimed, reaching towards him. Logan rubbed his forehead. "Ow! Gosh, Mitchell I thought your strength was in your legs! That was one mean, ow, punch." Holly frowned. "Will you stop with your crummy little jokes! You're here in the middle of a forest, with a very hurt face…and you're still going around with your jokes?" Logan tried to smile. "Hey, my jokes never stop." He tried to get up, but groaned. Holly rolled her eyes. "Oh, let me help you!" She said, helping him up. "Do you need like, ice or something?" Holly asked. "Not that I actually have any." Logan shook his head. "I don't think so. I mean, being a football player, you kinda get used to this stuff. But what I really need is to know where we are right now." Holly laughed, humourlessly. "Sorry, I can't help you with that. Cause, I don't know where we are either! I got distracted by some strange butterfly, and got lost." Logan raised an eyebrow. "Butterfly? Like with clear wings? Because that's exactly how I got lost." Holly nodded. "Wow, that's strange, isn't it?" She said. "But at the same time, nerve wracking! What are we going to do now? I mean, I'm pretty sure the others are way further ahead." Logan paced back and forth. "Well actually, if you think about it—"

"Wait, hold on!" Holly interrupted. "Did you hear that?" She looked around, suspiciously. "Hear what?" Logan remarked. A quiet crunch of leaves could be heard from nearby. Followed by another and another. "What is that?" Holly cried, nervously. Logan opened his mouth to say something, when the rustling came again, this time clearly coming from behind the trees. Holly sighed. "Let me guess, you're another one of the campers who got distracted by a magical butterfly and got lost, right? Well, you can come out of the tree now, because we're not foes. Come on, is that you curly haired girl? Or girl with a cool haircut? Ummm maybe one of the bffs? Or maybe someone I have not payed attention to?" Logan put a hand on Holly's shoulder. "Uhh, Holly I don't think it's someone from camp." He said, carefully. Holly turned to him slowly. "Then who could it be?" She whispered.

But that's when the being from behind the tree peeked out. Holly's eye's widened. It wasn't a person at all! In fact, it was a small pony. But not a regular one! It had a light pink coat, and a lavender mane with streaks of violet. It's eyes were the prettiest shade of emerald green, framed by long lashes. On its head, was a pink, glittery horn. Logan's eyes widened, looking at it up and down, with fascination and horror! But Holly? She couldn't believe what was in front of her! On top of it all, the pony(or was it…a unicorn???)

cleared its throat, and said awkwardly,"umm, hi. Sorry I didn't mean to freak you guys out or anything, I was just—"

"AHHHHH!" Holly screamed. Then everything went blank…

Holly's eyes slowly opened, when she felt water splashing on her face. Ohh where *am I?* She thought, trying to sit up. "Here let me help" said a sweet voice. Holly looked beside and saw a young girl, with dark skin, and curly hair, tied with a bandanna. She had a lovely and welcoming smile on her face. Holly rubbed her eyes. "W—where, where am I? Who are you?" She glared. "What am I doing here? What have you done with me? I can hardly move!" The girl kept smiling, and opened her mouth to say something, when a bubbly voice said, "here you go Kelly. I brought all the things you asked for." Holly recognized that voice. She turned and saw a glittery pony walking in, with some jars on her back. "I didn't have any sage left, so I had to go ask Gigi. Ohh and also, I couldn't find the rosemary anywhere. No one had any left, so Chuck went on back to get some." She kept babbling on, until her eyes met Holly's. "Oh, hey! You're awake!"

"You! I—I saw you in the forest! We, we got lost…and then…" She let the memories all fall back to place. Holly frowned, looking around what seemed to be a small house or hut. "But what am I doing here? I'm supposed to be in the forest…lost?" Now Holly was only confused. The girl smiled sympathetically. "Don't worry. You were in the in the forest with your friend. But then, umm." She turned to the unicorn, who finished for her. "Basically, after seeing me, you screamed, and then passed out. Then me and your friend brought you here. By the way, you were riding on my back." She bragged. Then looked embarrassed. "Well, half of the way here. Then the horse carried you to this cot." She says, glancing at the door.

Just then, they heard a laugh. Out of the corner, came Logan holding a small boy, about 5 or 6 and laughing. He saw Holly and grinned. "Oh, hey Holly! How are you feeling now?" He asked coming over and putting the boy down. He had a head full of brown curly hair, and the most adorable face ever. Holly shrugged. "Umm, better I guess. But my arms and legs feel like heavy rocks." Logan thrust his hand in his pockets. "You kinda did have a big fall, so can't say I'm surprised." Holly rolled her eyes. "But, um, if you guys don't mind me asking… Where exactly am I and who are you?" She asked politely.

The unicorn answered first. "Hi I'm Ophelia the Unicorn! Sorry I freaked you guys out earlier!' Holly tried to smile. "It's fine. It's just not everyday you see a colourful talking unicorn." Ophelia giggled. The little boy gasped. "You've never seen a talking animal before? Wow, you should go outside!" He laughed. The girl shook her head. "My name is Kelly. And this little guy right here is my brother Jessi." Jessi waved. "Hi!" He said, cheerfully. "Nice to meet you all, I guess. I'm Holly. And I'm sure you've met…" "Logan!" Jessi yelped, as Logan reached down to pick him up. "Logan, let's go visit the waterfall. Please?" Jessi begged. Logan laughed. "Alright little dude, let's go. You guys don't need anything else for Holly do you?" He asked. Kelly shook her head. So, Logan and Jessi went.

"Wow they've really bonded." Holly commented. Kelly nodded. "Yeah they have. Our parents passed away a long time ago and we had nowhere to go. Once, we got stranded in this forest, and honestly, that's the best thing that's happened to both of us, because we found an amazing home here. All the animals and people that lived here, took care of us and treated us just like their own. We've never had a moment where we thought we had no one left. So in return, I heal the animals and people here. I'm kind of the "doctor" here, except I don't have a degree or anything." She shrugged. "I'm so sorry." Holly said. "But um, you guys haven't really told me where "here" is." Kelly and Ophelia smiled. "Why don't you come see for yourself?" The little unicorn said, hopping to the door as Kelly helped Holly up. They reach the door and when Ophelia opened it eagerly, Holly's jaw dropped.

In front of her was a magnificent sight. Tall green trees, a small, sparkling river, tiny brown straw huts here and there, and lastly a majestic waterfall in the distance. But the most amazing sight of all, were the people walking around with baskets, kids playing games and animals running around, some with small children riding on their backs. There were bears, birds, horses, monkeys even a few tigers and lions, all walking freely among humans. So peaceful, calm.

While Holly was too busy admiring the wonders, a big brown bear walked up to the trio. "Hi guys. Here's the rosemary you asked me to bring, Ophelia." He said in a deep voice. "You can talk!" Holly yelped. Then shook her head. "Oh wait. Let me guess, all you animals can talk?" Kelly nodded, as the bear chuckled. A deep, friendly sound. Ophelia grinned wildly. "Yup! All the animals here can talk!" She gestured towards the bear. "This big guy is Chuck. Seems big and scary, but super friendly." Chuck smiled. "Hello. You must be the kid that passed out in the forest right?" Holly blushed. "Yeah, that's me. I'm Holly." Chuck laughed. "Oh it's nothing to be embarrassed about. My friend Cory always faints when he sees a basket full of yummy carrots." A bunny who happened to be hopping by, stopped. "Oh come on Chuck, I'm right here." He shot, slightly annoyed. He glared and quickly hopped off. Chuck laughed and started after him. "Sorry, I gotta go and apologize to good old Mr. Cory here. See you Ophelia. Bye Kelly. And a pleasure meeting you Holly." He says as he walks over to Cory.

Holly sighed. "Wow, this place is amazing! Talking animals that are super friendly, and an amazing, amazing landscape. It's so, magical!"

Kelly stretched her arms out, and faced Holly. "Welcome, to Crystal Clearing!"

PART TWO

A Mysterious Past

After Kelly had given Holly an herbal drink(which was supposed to help with pain), and after a small snack of veggie salad, it was already past noon. Holly didn't mind that she was missing the camping trip at all. In fact, she was kind of glad that the mysterious butterfly had lead her here. Apart from meeting some of the nicest people (and animals!), Holly learned that there was cell reception. Like full reception. She wanted to call Latisha and tell her about this wonderful place, but something told her not to.

A little feeling inside her gut. So she decided to scroll through her phone instead.

After a minute though, she got board. She hadn't seen Logan at all after she had woken up, unless that little slip of time when he was with Jessi. Ophelia had gone home, and Kelly was outside, picking vegetables, so she had no one to talk to. Holly got up from the little cot, and went outside. A soft breeze blew her blond hair sideways. Holly started walking, admiring everything. She passed by some people with baskets full of fruits and vegetables. She also passed by many animals, who eyed her curiously, but still smiled cheerful.

She hadn't walked far when something rolled past her foot. It was a soccer ball! She quickly ran towards it, and blocked it from going any further. "Over here!" Someone called. Holly looked up and saw a bunch of kids standing by a grassy field. One of them was waving his hands. Holly looked at the soccer ball, then at Kelly, still picking vegetables. *Oh well, Kelly won't mind if I have a little fun, would she?* She smiled and jogged over to the kids. "Hey, you guys mind if I join your game? I am pretty good at soccer!" The kid that was waving smiled. "Sure! You can be on our team, since we're short one player." A tiger on the sidelines, whistled. "Alright, we're starting from the beginning now, so ball in the middle!" She ordered. Then turned to Holly. "Ok, newbie! Let's go over some rules. I want a clean game, no cheating. Everyone's included and lastly the most important rule of all…" The tiger's glare turned into a grin as she said, "is to have fun!!!! You got that newbie?" Holly nodded.

The game started and Holly expertly kicked the ball towards the goalie. She passed to some other kids, and when they were finally near the net, they let Holly do the honours. One kick and in the ball went! Everyone cheered. "Oh my tiger tales, that was amazing!" The tiger shouted from the sidelines. Holly grinned wildly. She was enjoying every moment of this…

Holly didn't realize that hours had gone by, but by the time the Coach Daisy whistled, it was already dark. Everyone patted her on the back, saying she did great! Coach walked up to her. "Oh boy, kid. That was one of the most amazing games I've seen in my whole life, being a coach. I want you on my team!" Holly smiled. "I would love to!" She blurted. Coach Daisy patted her leg. "Now go get yourself a good nights sleep, we're practicing tomorrow evening." She said walking away. "I'll be there!" Holly called.

A bit tired, she jogged off the field where she saw a small crowd of people. "Woah! There she is, like the most amazing team player in, like, this whole clearing." Said a little parrot, perched on top of a monkey, who looked ready to run around the whole field wildly. "We we're watching you play the whole time and you were amazing! No brilliant! Awesome!" The monkey kept saying these as he ran off, screaming, shouting and laughing.

Holly giggled and turned to see who else was there. To her surprise, Ophelia, Kelly, Chuck and even Logan, holding Jessi were there. Everyone looked happy. "Wow! That was so fun to watch! I never cared much for watching soccer, but this was so cool!!" Ophelia chattered on.

Chuck gave Holly a high five. "Nice work, kiddo!" "Thanks!" Holly replied, taking a sip of water Kelly had brought. Kelly smiled. "That was nice Holly, but you should go and take some rest. Sleep. It's getting late, and if you don't take rest your whole body will ache." She says gently, taking the bottle back. Holly nodded, feeling ready to climb under warm blankets. "Yeah, i think I'm going to go in soon. But, where am I going to sleep?" She asked, rubbing her eyes. "You can sleep on the cot. Don't worry Jessi and I have are own cots. And Logan, you can sleep on the spare hammock in Jessi's room. I'll find you guys some extra blankets." Holly and Logan eyed each other. "Sorry for your inconvenience, Kelly. We don't mean to be a disturbance." Holly said, blushing. Kelly smiled, genuinely. "Don't worry about it. We don't get visitors much, so I'm just happy!" She said, slowly dragging Jessi away from Logan, and heading down the field. Chuck and Ophelia followed close behind. "Good night! See you!" They said.

Holly cleared her throat. "Um, so I assume you had a nice time with Jessi? I mean, you *were* with him for the whole day, almost!" She pretended to examine a leafy plant close by. Logan smiled. "Oh yeah, it was great! Jessi showed me the whole place. And he even introduced me to some people. And some animals as well. They are all so friendly! Have you met any of them yet?" Holly nodded. "Yeah, kind of. I know Chuck and Ophelia, of course. And I met their friend Cory and his sister Gigi, too. Oh, I can't forget Daisy. She's the tiger, and the soccer coach. So far, everyone I met—people or animals—are super nice!" Logan eagerly grinned. "I know right? It's so cool how humans and animals live alongside each other so peacefully."

Suddenly a far away look crossed his face. "You know, the fun I had with Jessi today reminds me of when we used to play together. Do you remember? We would always play tennis together, or watch sci-fi movies at each other's houses." He laughed at the memory. Holly flinched, letting the memories fall back. Logan sadly looked Holly in the eye. "Holly, why did you—" "Oh, yawn yawn, goodness I am so tired right now! Uh, um, you know what, I think I'm gonna go, and sleep, I mean go to sleep! I gotta go to sleep. So, um, bye see you tomorrow! It—it was amazing talking with you! Uh, good night! Bye." She grinned awkwardly, and walked away as fast as her legs could, without waiting for Logan to say anything. *No! I can't talk about this right now! I just can't!*

She came near Kelly's hut and when she got inside, she saw that Kelly had put a handmade quilt and pillow on the cot. Holly could hear faint snoring coming from the back. *Kelly and Jessi are probably asleep.* She yawned and went over to the cot. Within seconds, she fell into a deep, dreamless sleep.

Holly woke to the sound of chatter. She rubbed her eyes and sat up. Ophelia and Chuck were in the corner chatting. Ophelia saw Holly and brightly said, "Good morning! Oh, sorry did we wake you?" Holly shook her head and smiled. "No, in fact you guys woke me up just in time. I think I slept in. Like for a long time." She bent underneath the cot and pulled out her duffel bag. "Ohh nice bag!" Ophelia eagerly walked up, Chuck following. Holly pulled out her phone to check the time. "10:30?! Oh goodness, I definitely slept in!" She exclaimed. Chuck looked curiously at the phone. "If you don't mind me asking, what's that?" He asked in his deep, yet friendly voice. Ophelia shook her head. "Oh, Chuck! It's called a *cell phone.* Haven't you ever seen the humans that walk in the forests clicking away on them?" She put a pretend serious look on her face. Chuck just smiled. "Oh, I didn't know you were starting to become just like Violet the parrot." Ophelia raised an eyebrow. "Oh? And what's that supposed to mean?" "That you spy on people, walking past our clearing"

He says, calmly. Ophelia snorts. "Spying? On people? Did I say that? I didn't say that! Did I?" Holly and Chuck exchange knowing glances. The little unicorn rolled her eyes. "Ha Ha, very funny, you guys. Very funny." Holly giggled. She looked around. "Hey, where is everyone?" Chuck adjusted his cap. "Jessi woke up a bit sick, so Kelly's busy helping him. As for your friend, he said he was going for a walk. Left early in the morning. Hasn't come back yet."

Just then, they heard a cough coming from the back. It sounded rough and dry. "Oh no! Jessi doesn't sound that well. I'm going to go and check on him." Holly said worriedly, putting on her sneakers. She stood up and shivered. "Oh wow, it's cold here!" She commented, putting her hands into her pockets. "Even with a warm hoodie on." Chuck nodded. "Yeah, even with fur as thick as this Im feeling the cold." Ophelia frowned. "That's strange! Usually it's perfect here. Not too cold, not too hot."

Suddenly, the sound of thunder roared outside. Ophelia yelped and jumped behind Chuck. Thick, heavy rain could be heard, followed by bits of thunder. Ophelia gulped. "Chuck, w—what's happening? There's never a thunderstorm here! And sure there's rain, but never like this!" Chuck reached down to pat the nervous unicorn, looking somewhat scared himself. Holly frowned. "Hey, maybe the rain—" she was cut off when the front door burst open and in came the monkey who had been at Holly's soccer game, screaming. "Kelly! Kelly come quick! Felix's going crazy! Help! Kelly!" He screamed, waving his hands wildly. "Rocky, what's wrong?" Ophelia and Chuck ran over as Holly followed. Rocky's eyes grew wide, as he pointed outside, where a large horse was causing a tantrum. Kicking and neighing violently. Coach Daisy was trying to control it, along with a few other strong looking animals.

Kelly came running from the room, her long red skirt swirling around her. "What happened?" She asked, worriedly. "It's Felix! He's going crazy again! Just like a few days ago!" Rocky screeched, waving his hands in the direction. Kelly's big green eyes grew alarmed. "Again? Oh, no!" She looked at Ophelia. "Ophelia, go get my sage and thyme herbal mix! Now! In the wooden jar!" Kelly ordered. Ophelia ran. "Chuck, give me a boost!" Chuck sceptically lowered himself as

Kelly climbed on. "Violet!" She called to a little parrot flying nearby. "Slingshot, please."

Ophelia came back with a jar in her mouth and Violet the bird flew back with a wooden slingshot. "Come on guys, you can do it! Just hold him in place for a bit longer!" Ophelia encouraged, to the animals holding Felix in place. Kelly aimed the slingshot and then, BAM! The green paste fell straight to his mouth. In an instant, Felix calmed, almost hypnotized. Then, as if on cue, Daisy and the others moved to the sides, as Felix took a great fall. Kelly though, jumped off Chuck's back, and called orders to some other animals.

Seeing Holly's mortified expression, Ophelia whispered, "um, just in case you wanted to know... Felix is the one who carried you here, when you fainted in the forest yesterday. Just thought you could use a little energy booster." She laughed nervously. Holly exhaled. "Um, good to know. I guess." She tried to smile.

From the corner of her eye, she saw Logan running towards them. "Guys! Are you ok? Did you see what happened to Felix?" He asked in a hurry. Holly could only nod her head.

Just then, Chuck came out, his face unusually serious. "Ophelia, I really think we ought to tell them, now. I mean, this is the second time this has happened and if we don't do anything now, then who knows what's going to be next?" Ophelia eyed them, still looking nervous. "Tomorrow, it could be you! Or me, turning into violent creatures." Ophelia sighed. "You're right Chuck. They already saw what happened, so I think we can tell them now." Chuck nodded. "But one of us has to stay here and help Kelly. Here I'll stay with her, and you go explain." "Wait, you want me to tell them myself? No way, Chuck you're staying with me! And besides look, there's many people here with Kelly. I see Rocky and Violet, Cory and Gigi, Daisy, even the lion twins. Everyone in the Clearing is here! Together they can all help Felix and Jessi!" Ophelia gestured inside. "Fine! Just let me go tell Kelly." The bear reluctantly said.

While they were talking, Holly and Logan cluelessly stared. "Um, are they talking about us, by any chance?" Logan leans in and whispers. Holly shrugged. "I think so? I don't know. I'm completely clueless right now!" Holly replied. Ophelia looked at them, blinking. "Uh, Ophelia what's happening?" Holly asked, concerned. "Nothing!" Ophelia says, a little too loudly. "But um, let's step away for a moment." She says, pushing them towards the pouring rain. "In the rain?" Holly says, trying to cover herself. "No! Under that mango tree!" Ophelia urged, pushing them quickly. "Mango tree?" Logan says, looking around. Ophelia starts laughing awkwardly. "Did I say mango tree? Whoopsie! I meant willow tree! Yeah willow tree, that's it." Holly and Logan eyed each other. "Ophelia are you ok?" Holly asks, as they reached the mysterious tree, which was further away from the huts. Now, Ophelia's eye is twitching. "Listen, I don't mean to be rude or anything, but if we needed to talk, couldn't we have done it inside the hut? Why all the way over here?" Logan irked. Ophelia's eye stopped twitching, and she sighed. "Because there's too much people in there." Now she looked sad. "Ophelia, seriously what's wrong?" Holly asked, concerned.

The unicorn took a deep breath, as Chuck joined them under the tree. They give each other a look and then, everything starts pouring out of her mouth. "So, firstly, you know how I first met you in the forest when you were lost?

There's actually a reason for that! It's not some coincidence!" She paused for a moment. "You guys both got lost, because of some pretty butterflies with crystal wings, right?" Holly's jaw dropped. "Wait, how did you know?" Logan asked, backing up. Ophelia looked right into their eyes. "Because you were destined to be here. Haven't you guys ever wondered, why all us animals can talk? Or how we live so peacefully among all the humans? Well, the answer is here! Under this willow tree." She motioned for them to follow her, as she walked to the other side of the tree. There, carved in the bark, was a golden tablet, shining dimly. It had four squares at the bottom, each with a symbol. A heart, a cloud, a human, and a cat. The cat symbol looked dark and burnt, unlike the rest.

Chuck stared at it sadly. "It used to shine brighter." He remarked. Holly looked at it with fascination. As she reached out to touch the tablet, it sparked violently, and the cloud image darkened, with it the rain falling even harder uncontrollably. "Wait, does this…control everything in the clearing?" Logan wondered. "Yes! It does! Each little square represents something special to the clearing." Chuck says, pointing. "The human symbol represents all the people that live here, and the cat represents all the animals here. This tablet keeps the relationship between the two, easygoing and peaceful." Ophelia continued on. "Just like that, the cloud symbol stands for the weather. Not too hot and not too cold, with perfect amounts of rain, sun and snow. But as you can see, the square is burnt out! Now the weather will be uncontrollable." She sighed. "The reason Felix was acting like a real, untamed horse was because of this. It was burned a couple days ago." No sooner had she said it, they heard a violent roar, and obnoxious rumbling.

Ophelia started crying, softly. "What about the heart square? What does that mean?" Holly asked gently. Chuck, who was busy comforting Ophelia, looked up. "It stands for love and peace among everything and everyone. If that burns out, then everything will be over!" Holly walked over to the tablet, closely examining it. "Who made this plaque? And also, you said that we were destined to be here? What's that supposed to mean?" Logan asked, raising his eyebrow. Ophelia and Chuck looked at each other. "Well, if you want to know everything about the plaque, and how you two play a role in all this, then I think you guys will be better of going to Luna" Chuck says.

"Luna?" Holly wondered. Chuck nodded. "Luna's the wisest and most respected member of this clearing. She's an old wolf who lives by herself, near the back of the forest. It's said that she has strange visions, but with those visions she keeps the Clearing safe. We have all heard the stories behind this plaque, but she's the keeper of the secret." Chuck peeked behind the tree. "I think you guys should go to her right now, because the situation here is not going to improve anytime soon." He looked at the unicorn. "Ophelia I think you should take them there. Someone has to stay and help Kelly. And besides, if I go with them and I happen to turn into my real, bear self, then—" he gulped. "I don't want to put these guys at risk." Ophelia blinked back tears. "You always put other other's safety first, don't you?" She sniffed, patting Chuck's furry leg. "Alright come on you two." She motioned for Holly and Logan to follow as Chuck made his way back.

Ophelia led them further from the willow tree and closer to the waterfall. "The flies that you saw on the way here, are called Crystal Flies.

They are very important creatures." Ophelia was saying, while walking. "They only fly to people who are special. I think you guys are going to save the clearing!" Her eyes glittered. Holly snorted on the inside. *Us? Save the clearing? Ha, that's the funniest thing I've heard!* But she couldn't say it in front of Ophelia. The poor unicorn's spirits were already crushed, so she just decided to stay quiet. Beside her Logan gulped, looking worried.

"Here we are!" They stopped in front of the crashing waterfall, with diamond like water. "Here we are where? Where's Luna?" Holly asked, looking around. "Oh, she not here, we have to go in, silly." Ophelia replied. "In the waterfall?! You're kidding right?" Logan yelps. He suddenly felt someone turning him around. Ophelia came up from behind saying, "not the waterfall, the cave!"

After a moment of silence, Logan laughed nervously. "You know, I think I prefer the waterfall." He backed up. Holly agreed. The cave beside the waterfall wasn't exactly welcoming. It looked like the kind of place where people went missing. Ophelia burst out laughing. "You guys, don't worry! Luna's not going to eat you guys alive! It's just that she lives by herself in a creepy dark cave. She's actually really wise. I went to see her when I was a wee pony." She wiped tears from her eyes. "Alright scaredy cats, let's go." She walked fearlessly into the dark cave. "Scaredy cats? Hey Logan, don't you have the greatest answers for these kind of remarks?" Holly asked jokingly."You know, I'm not even going to lie about not being scared, because I'm absolutely terrified right now!" Logan admitted, shivering.

Ophelia stopped and peered into a dark open space. "Luna, is that you? I brought some friends that you might want to meet." A murmur was heard, followed by a quick movement and a pair of golden eyes, appearing in the dark. A shaft opened, letting in sunlight. A wolf with silver fur and sharp ears was sitting by the shaft, looking strangely at Holly and Logan. Ophelia stepped forward. "A good morning to you Luna. I have a couple friends that you might want to meet." She says, with great calmness. The old wolf smiled mysteriously. "A good morning to you as well, Ophelia. Now who are your friends?" She asks. "This is Holly, and this is Logan. They're from the real world. They were in the forest, when the Crystal flies distracted them." Luna tilts her head. "Crystal flies, you say?" Ophelia nodded.

Luna eyed them. "Come closer, kids." She waved her paw. Holly and Logan looked at Ophelia. "Oh come now, I won't bite!" She laughed. They both cautiously walked over.

Just then, a butterfly like creature flew from the shaft, and began circling around the kids. Holly immediately recognized the flies that had led her to Crystal Clearing. A Crystal fly. The beautiful creature swirled around her and Logan. "Unbelievable!" Luna murmured, eyes wide. "You two really are the ones." "Um, the what?" Logan asked, confused. The old wolf got up and started walking towards them. "The ones who are going to save the clearing!" She replied. "I already told them about the Crystal flies on the way here." Ophelia spoke up. Luna nodded, a distant look crossing her face. "Listen Luna, I'm not trying to be rude or anything, but how are we supposed to save this clearing? It's impossible! We're just two normal kids with no magical powers." Holly shrugged. Luna's golden eyes glittered. "Ahh, but that is what you think, my dear children." She turned and made her way to the shaft slowly. "I'm not assuming you do have powers, but the crystal flies never lie." She turned her head back abruptly, a very serious look in her eyes. "Now children, you probably have not the slightest idea what I'm talking about. So, since the Crystal flies made it clear that you two are special, I will tell you everything. The whole history of how this magnificent Clearing came to be. Have a seat! This might take a while. Ophelia, you too." Holly and Logan nervously took a seat on the hard cave ground, as Ophelia joined them. Luna closed her eyes.

"Years ago, before Crystal Clearing came to be, this land was a rural village, where the people of Cobblestone Valley lived long ago. It was a calm village, seated near a dangerous forest, where wolves lived. These wolves would occasionally attack the villagers in packs, biting, growling and killing." Luna sighed, at this point. "So they all had to live in great caution. But other than that, everything was fine."

Luna slowly started walking around. "Then, in 1956, three little kids were born, at the same time. Primrose, Milo, and Clementine. Primrose was eldest, followed by Clementine. Milo was born a few minutes later. Primrose and Milo became great friends. But Clementine preferred to keep to herself. Of course, the other kids tried including her in games, but she wasn't really a people person. Anyways, the kids in that village, had serious rules regarding the forest of wolves. They were not allowed to set foot near the area. But tragically one day, in 1966 when a wolf attack was taking place, poor Milo was caught in between and mauled by the wolves. Upon finding his dead body laying on the ground, Primrose was deeply saddened. Now, Milo had always been an animal lover and longed to see a world where humans and animals lived peacefully. He had always vowed that when he was older, he would make that happen somehow. With that thought in mind, Primrose shut herself in her room and cried for days, wishing she could make his dreams come true."

Luna paused, eyeing Holly, Logan, and Ophelia, who all happened to be speechless. She closed her eyes and continued. "No one knows exactly how she did it, but it's said that her tears and sadness mixed with her love for Milo, created the golden plaque. Then one day, she ventured out into the forest and found a willow tree. She sat underneath it and placed the plaque on the ground. She was saying how this was going to change the world. In a way, she was talking to Milo, hoping he could be seeing this and smiling.

But then, Clementine appeared from behind a tree." Luna abruptly turned around, facing them.

"Apparently, Clementine had followed Primrose into the forest. And mistakenly, after hearing what Primrose had said about the plaque saving the world, Clementine was filled with rage and more importantly, jealousy! She misunderstood, thinking that Primrose had made the plaque to show off. You see, Primrose and Milo were quite popular in the village, for being friends. Clementine, since she was distant from everyone else, grew envious of them both. After Milo died and Primrose shut herself down, Clementine was just so angry as she thought Primrose was grieving for attention. She was tired of being unseen." Luna sighed.

"Primrose tried telling her she was mistaken, but of course Clementine wouldn't listen. But right at that moment, a pack of wolves rounded the forest and caught sight of Clementine and Primrose. They started running towards them, before the girls could do anything. The wolves ended up killing poor Primrose. As they were about to pounce on Clementine, she realized something. All these years she had never really felt home in the village. She saw these wolves and was instantly drawn to them. She saw them as a better community than the villagers. The wolves didn't try mauling her. In fact, they turned back into the woods, almost motioning the girl to follow. Clementine looked at the plaque lying on the ground with a few cracks, and thought that since it was all ruined, Primrose's plan would never work. But as she disappeared into the forest with the wolves, the broken plaque shone brightly, repairing all the cracks itself. There was so much light that a little boy who accidentally ran into the forest while playing with his friends, saw it. As he went near, the plaque's power began to glow." Luna paused for minute.

"The ground began shaking, the wind blew hard. But after, there was a great calm. That's when the plaque's power began. The animals that had been living in the forest began to cross into the village and everyone's minds were filled with tolerance and acceptance. Everyone, people and animals, were changed." Luna looked at them sadly.

"Everyone except the wolves. You see, some were changed, but many, due to their negativity, couldn't be changed. Clementine, under influence of the wolves, ran far away. Away from all this positivity."

Luna walked closer to them. "I've been having visions lately. The same one over and over. It shows our clearing engulfed in flames. I hear a faint howl and then, a yellow rose falls on the fire, silencing the howls and screams. Then a lotus falls causing the fire to slowly disappear. From my vision, one thing is clear. The fire was started by wolves. Not just any, but the bad ones." Luna stopped and there was silence.

Holly finally had the courage to speak. "But, I—If they wanted to attack, couldn't they have done so right when everything started?" Luna nodded. "Yes, they could have. But they wanted to see how long we would stay put. If I remember correctly, when I was young wolf, I would often see the the elders and leaders discussing something about attacking when we least expected. They were waiting perhaps, for a golden opportunity and then they would take it all away from us." Luna looked sad. "I know what you kids are thinking. Why am I, a wolf, here talking to you. Well, my father was one of the elders, but he, alongside my mother and a couple other wolves were against all this violence done by my pack. But when the others found out that my father wasn't a supporter of them, they threatened to kick him out of the council. When he refused…they killed him." Her voice choked.

"Ever since that incident none of us dared to speak up. Some tried running away, but they would be beaten to death. It was at that moment, some of us realized, that this pack we once loved, was filled with evil, violent wolves. When the power of the plaque had been released, some of us wolves were influenced by it, you see. The elders kicked us out of the village and told us to get lost. We were happy, but then some of us started getting sick and only then did we realize that the elders had cast a spell on us."

Luna stared at the shaft a distant look crossing her face. "Soon my parents died. But I had miraculously survived. I ran into the Clearing, and the animals and people here took me in. With my visions I managed to keep the Clearing safe all these years. But I don't know if I can now that everything is messed up." Her ice blue eyes glittered. "My biggest fear is that the pack will now come back."

Holly and Logan stared wide eyed. Ophelia's jaw was wide open. Luna was about to say something, when the Crystal flies began hovering over Holly and Logan rapidly. They then, flew over to two rocks in the cave flying around them, moving them together. They then flew to Ophelia buzzing around her ferociously. "W—what's going on? What happened to the Crystal flies?" Ophelia cried, just as the creatures flew near the cave opening flying faster then anything they had ever seen before. Luna gasped. "I—I think that the Crystal flies have been affected by all the havoc!" She exclaimed. "But I thought you said the Crystal flies never lie." Logan whispered, confused. Luna sighed, as she watched the flies, who seemed to be calming down now. "I'm afraid that nothing is certain. We can't trust anything anymore." She croaked, tearfully. The Crystal flies once again fluttered around the cave stopping from Holly to Logan to Ophelia and Luna.

Luna turned to them and bowed her head. "We can't trust them anymore. I had always thought that nothing would affect them, but… of course, I was wrong." Ophelia blinked back tears. "Does—does that mean that Holly and Logan aren't going to be the ones to save the Clearing?" The little unicorn asked. "I'm afraid so, Ophelia." The old wolf started gently. "The animal square of the plaque burnt out days ago, and I had noticed them flying around anxiously lately. They probably flew to your friends unknowingly."

Luna now turned to Holly and Logan. "I apologize kids, for putting pressure on you. I'm glad you got to know the history of the Clearing, but unfortunately it's no use now." She bowed her head in remorse. Holly and Logan looked at each other. Then back at Luna. "It's ok. We're really sorry this is happening to the Clearing. We really wish we could help." Holly says emphatically. Logan spoke up. "Maybe we could stay for a couple more days and help you guys out? It's the least we could do." Luna smiled weakly. "You kids have kind hearts. But I can't have you two get hurt. You are guests at our Clearing and should not have to be forced to do anything." Holly and Logan stood there silently. Luna bowed her head. "It was an absolute pleasure meeting you two. Thank you for all your offerings. I appreciate it very much. Farewell. Farewell Ophelia." With that she disappeared into the dark cave.

Ophelia led them out. The walk back was silent. No one dared to say a word. But when the trio started nearing the huts, that was almost impossible because although the storm had stopped, the chaos around them had grown worse. Some were trying to restrain a lion, a few animals looked really cranky, people where coughing. But along with all that, something new had popped up while they were gone.

A nearby man was wiping mud off his steps. "Stupid bunny!" He muttered. A second later, Cory the bunny came. "Hi Jack. Just here to get some carrots, like usual." He started, about to go in. But the man (Jack) stopped him. "Woah! Hold up, Cory. You see all this mud that I'm cleaning up? This is from you! All of it! So, from now on, you must clean your feet before you come. Otherwise you won't get any carrots." He says, sternly. Cory frowns. "What happened to you Jack? Usually you don't even care about this stuff." Jack folds his arms. "What happened is I'm starting to care about my house." "Well, guess what Jack? I don't have dainty little foot coverings like yours. They don't make any for my hoppers." Cory steps closer. "And also, when did this become *your* house? I live with you too, you know." "If you don't have foot coverings then go get some from Bianca. She makes all our clothes. I'm sure she can make a pair for your clown feet!" Cory gasps. "Ohh no you did not just say that! Take it back, stick feet!" And the two began arguing, calling each other names.

"The plaque!" Ophelia, Holly and Logan all say at the same time. They ran to the Willow tree and sure enough, the human square was looking dimmer then usual. "Oh no! It's going to burn out soon! And then after that, the heart square is going to burn out and, and, and then, ohh" she dropped to the ground, crying. Holly and Logan quickly tried comforting her. "Its ok Ophelia, don't cry. Um, I have some chocolate in my bag, you've always wanted to try chocolate right? Uhh, want me to go get some?" Logan tried. Holly shot him a look. "Logan this isn't joke time! Can't you see someone's here crying?" Ophelia wiped her tears and looked up. Her emerald eyes grew wide as she called out, "Chuck!" Holly and Logan turned as they saw a silhouette of the bear running towards them in the distance. "Ophelia, what happened at Luna's? And why are you crying?" He asked, coming near her. Ophelia kept crying, so Holly explained everything that had happened at the old wolf's cave.

"Oh no!" Chuck said, after she had finished. "And that's not all." Logan began. "We saw a guy named Jack arguing with your friend Cory. He was getting mad at Cory for getting his house dirty and then they started calling each other names. After seeing that, we came to check the plaque and…" his voice trailed off as Chuck examined it only to gasp. "Oh no! Now all the humans are going to act selfish and intolerant." He sighed. "So, did anything else happen while we were gone?" Holly asked, kneeling down. Chuck shook his furry head. "Other then a few animals going mad and a bit of heavy rain, nothing else." He rubbed his eyes. He looked tired.

Ophelia was now staring at the sky, which had turned dark surprisingly soon. Holly looked up as well. Millions of twinkling stars looked down at her, and for once, a great calmness seemed to drift over the group. Until they heard a loud, thunderous sound followed by flashing lightning…

PART THREE

Friendship forever

Holly couldn't sleep that night. She tossed and turned, unable to rest. So, instead of trying anymore, she got up and went outside. Things had gotten back to normal by then and everyone had gone to sleep peacefully.

She sat on the steps admiring the wonderful place she had been in for the last couple days. Even in the darkness, Crystal Clearing had a magical glow. A cold wind blew, making Holly shiver. She smiled, recalling moments when she and Logan would have sleepovers and sneak off to the porch in the middle of the night, telling stories and making jokes and eventually falling asleep there, only to get an earful from their parents. Holly giggled. "Well, looks like I'm not the only one who can't fall asleep." Said a voice behind her. She didn't need to turn around to recognize who's voice it was. "Oh, hi Logan."

Logan sat on the steps beside Holly. "So, what's been on your mind?" He asked. Holly rolled her eyes. "What do you think is on my mind, Logan?" She picked up a small rock. "The fact that we got whisked away to this magical, peaceful land, for starters. Then its the fact that all this peacefulness is slowly creeping away." She sighed. "I wish we could do something for them." Holly glanced at Logan, who seemed to be lost in his thoughts, staring into the dark yet charming Clearing. "Hey! Logan!" She says, which makes him jump. "Did you hear anything I said?" Logan shook his head sheepishly. "Sorry, I was just thinking about…you know, the plaque and all." He frowned. "Wait a minute, do you think that the reason the plaque is burning out is because Clementine and the wolves are near the Clearing?" Holly thought about it. "Actually, you could be right. They could be waiting for the plaque to burn out completely before they attack."

Suddenly, Holly felt a shiver run down her spine. She was scared, not much for herself, but for the inhabitants of Crystal Clearing.

Just then, she heard a howl in the distance. It wasn't just any howl though. It was a wolf howl! Logan stood up fast. "Uh oh, it looks like their not going to wait for the plaque to burn out!" The howl came again, but this time more clearer and louder, followed by a chorus of barks. The animals weren't in sight, but they were nearing.

Holly and Logan quickly woke Kelly and Jessi up. They all ran and woke up everyone else in the Clearing. Everyone seemed frightened. Holly raced to the last hut, and escorted the family out. But they had just taken a few steps when they heard the howls. Only this time, it was coming from inside the Clearing. Holly whisked around to find a terrifying sight. A pack of hungry, vicious looking wolves stood, with wicked expressions on their evil, furry faces.

A single howl came from the back, and all the wolves howled in reply, moving to the sides to form a pathway. Lightning roared through the sky as 2 silhouettes, one of a wolf and the other of a human, started walking forward. As they got closer, the inhabitants of Crystal Clearing could make out a large creepy wolf with silver fur and some sort of crystal object hung around their neck, alongside a woman with curly, messy orange hair and wearing what looked like the remains of an old fashioned girl's dress, with was torn and had scratches. But the most terrifying of all was her body. There was grey fur running through her arms and legs, as well as part of her face, the other side revealing wrinkly skin. One of her threatening eyes was a crystal blue and the other was golden, just like the other wolves. Holly gasped at the figure. She felt like running away, and disappearing. Logan also seemed shocked, along with the other village folks, who stood there speechless. Holly felt like she was going to pass out, but at that moment, she spotted something on the lady's head. They were a pair of wolf ears.

Seeing that, she backed up, a hand on her head, trying to stop a blistering migraine. Migraines were something she got often, following a really bad head concussion when she was 6. They usually happened when she was stressed, scared or panicked. Like *really* panicked.

Just like the time she cried in the bathroom, knowing Logan would never be her friend again.

Holly exhaled trying to keep the pain mild while also trying to pay attention to what was going on. By now the wolf smiled slyly. "Good day, village folk." He began in a voice dripping with greed. "Allow me to introduce myself and my companion here." He looked at each of the village folk in the eye, and when his eyes laid on Logan and Holly, they seemed to rest on them longer than anyone else. "My name is Alister and I'm the alpha of this pack. And this," He says nodding towards the lady, "is my trusty sidekick… Clementine." Alister stretched out the name. Many villagers gasped. Holly, wide eyed, also gasped. *So this is Clementine. Oh no, they've turned her half wolf!* Holly quickly put her hands back on her head. The pain was only getting worse, and her vision was starting to blur a bit.

Alister started walking around. "What? There's no introduction from all of you?" He laughed, an ugly sound. "Oh It's fine, I won't take it personally." His eyes narrowed. "Because I know exactly who you are. Clementine, would you like to explain?" He motioned to the wolf lady. She stepped forward and began talking in a raspy voice. "You all are the happy creatures who live in this magical forest, created by none other then my attention seeking neighbour, Primrose and her little pawn, Milo, who both sadly passed away years ago." She stated in mock sadness. Holly's vision got back to normal again, but she felt a distant ringing in her ears. *Oh god, I hate the ringing!* She thought.

Meanwhile, Alister cackled. "Yes, exactly, and you even reminded them of their history. Oh Clementine, what would I do without you?" He stopped laughing, instantly, and growled. "I genouresly gave you 50 years of freedom, waiting for the perfect chance, And now you are all mine!" He shouted, about to lunge towards the crowd, but at that moment, a voice shouted, "Stop!" The ring in Holly's ears ceased immediately. Although she didn't hear anything Alister had said, Holly saw Luna run towards the scene.

Alister's eyes turned cold. "Luna! I should have known it was you protecting the people." He said mockingly. Luna growled. "I will not let you hurt these people. I've protected them all these years and I shall keep doing so. After all, they took me in, when you kicked me out.

I found a better home in this Clearing, then in your untrustworthy pack, where you do nothing but brainwash everyone." Alister looked at Luna, blazing with fury. "I thought doing away with your father was the way to go. But obviously, I was wrong! I should have wiped you out first!" He howled loudly and then something that looked like electrifying blue lightning shot from his eyes. Holly, Logan and almost all the village folk gasped, frightened. Holly's migraine which had been absent for a couple seconds returned.

But Luna dodged it and sent her own electrifying lightning in Alister's way. Alister growled. Holly glanced at Logan, looking more panicked then ever. Right beside him, a frightened Kelly, who was usually so calm, was comforting sobbing Jessi. Holly looked to her other side, where Ophelia was buried in Chuck's furry body. Even Chuck himself looked confused and scared, while petting the tearful unicorn. Holly wanted so desperately to help these people and see a smile on all their faces. Her thoughts were shaken up when Luna, still fighting with Alister yelled, "Everyone! Quickly, run away! Don't worry about me, I'll be fine. Save yourselves!"

The village folk reluctantly started moving across the Clearing. Holly stood there looking between Luna and the entrance. "But—but, w—hat about Luna, she's, she…" Holly stammered, confused and feeling dizzy. Logan grabbed her hand. "Holly come on, we have to go! No one wants to leave them alone, but we have to. At least Luna has some kind of power! We don't have anything! Let's go!" He pulled Holly with him, but stopped in his tracks.

It didn't matter if they went or not now, because the entrance was blocked. Hundreds of wolves were guarding the entrance, with Clementine at the centre, sneering. The village folk stood there, unsure what to do. Everyone had been too focused on Luna and Alister, that they didn't see the rest of the pack sliding away to block the entrances. Alister cackled. "So, you thought you could protect them forever, am I right Luna?" His eyes turned a dangerous blue and the blue lightning grew stronger. Luna tried battling against it, but it was too strong. So strong that Luna failed to contain it. It struck her and sent her flying towards a tree.

"Luna!" a boy called, trying to run to her, but tripping on the paw of a wolf that sneaked it's way behind him. The wolf pinned him down. Coach Daisy runs to try and help him, but also gets held down. They scream helplessly. Holly and Logan so desperately wanted to help them, but it was no use. They would be attacked by the wolves. The wolves were too strong. Luna weakly tried getting up. But Alister ran and pinned her down as well, making her unable to move at all. Holly felt like she was going to pass out again. Logan looked at Luna and sighed. The village folk were murmuring, kids were crying, animals were growling, it was a terrifying sight.

While Alister was busy wresting Luna, Clementine began speaking in her raspy voice. "Ahhh, the life of your wise princess is in grave turmoil, but let's not worry about that now. Alister has it all covered. We have more important things to worry about. Like all of your lives." A firefly buzzed past her, but she grabbed it and crushed it. The people gasped. She laughed. "Scared? Well, guess what? This day, all of your lives will go POOF, crushed and in pain like this little fly." Her eyes landed on Holly and Logan. "Now, before I get to all that, let's talk about some newcomers." Logan and Holly eyed each other. Could Clementine be talking about them?

The wolf lady slowly started walking. "We were planning to have a surprise attack in the middle of the night. Attacking when you least expected us to. There's always an extra thrill to that. But unfortunately, 2 newcomers or shall I say guests, who have an extremely, extremely keen sense of hearing rained on our parade."

When she finished, she was standing right in front of Holly and Logan. Before they could do anything, Clementine snapped her fingers and two wolves lunged at them, knocking the kids to the ground. "Get off us!" Holly wrestled in vain. Logan tried hitting him, but the wolf was unbelievably strong. Even a trained football player or wrestler couldn't tackle these wolves.

Some Village folk tried helping. Chuck ran over and grabbed Holly's hand pulling her, while a lion tried helping Logan. Cory and Gigi used their giant bunny feet to push and kick them off. Felix used his horse strength to kick them out of the way. Rocky climbed on top of a wolf, pulling it's ears, only to be thrown to the ground. Ophelia ran and poked a wolf's back with her horn. But another wolf pounced on her, causing her to scream. All the people and animals tried helping, but it was just no use. All the wolves pounced on them, strangling, pinning them down, and wrestling.

The wolves holding Holly and Logan down, grabbed their feet with their sharp teeth and pulled them. Holly groaned in pain. Logan squirmed around. The wolves threw them in front of a tree, their heads hitting the trunk hard. They sat there weak and dazed. Clementine appeared before them with a dark black triangular rock in hand. "Since you two are the ones who rained on our parade, I'll prepare a front row seat for you, to feast your eyes on all this destruction. You newcomers will be the last to perish, but when you do…you will die a painful death." Holly and Logan broke out of the daze, hearing this. Logan got up, pulling Holly and tried to run. But just as he had taken the first stride, Clementine dropped the eerie rock and it burst into fire, creating a ring around the whole tree.

"No!" Logan shouted. "Yes!" Clementine shouted back. She snickered mockingly. "Have fun, guests! I'll be back to check on you in, let's say 20 minutes. Sound good?" She kept snickering while the wolves howled. Holly collapsed to the ground a hand on her head, blistering with an unbearable migraine. "Oh gosh, I forgot about your migraine problem. Are you ok?" Holly was taken aback. "You—you still remember?" Logan rolled his eyes. "Of course I do. How can I forget? You got a terrible one when we went to that amusement park, remember? You were doing just fine until you went on that slingshot ride. You were freaked out." He shrugged. "I guess I was too, though." Holly thought back to those happy moments. The migraine stopped for a couple seconds.

She thought about the rides and snacks. The sound of the crackling fire brought her back to reality. "Oh my gosh." She started, jumping up. "What are we going to do? How are we going to get out of here?" Holly turned and saw the tree. "Maybe we can climb on top of the tree?" Logan shook his head. "That won't work. It's too hard to climb up all the way there and even if we do, we can't jump down." Holly saw the fire ring closing into a circle. In a few more minutes, they would burn and die. The thought of that made Holly want to just disappear.

But then, through the large flames, she saw something that made her want to disappear even more. It was Crystal Clearing. The beautiful place had been replaced with dark, eerie skies, and chaos. She heard howls, screams and children crying. And in a corner there was blood, splattered all over the ground. She couldn't take it anymore. She ran to the other side of the tree and limply sat down arms wrapped around her legs. She felt her eyes getting watery. She had never been a crier, but that sight just made her want to cry hard.

"Holly, is everything ok?" Logan asks, gently. Holly looked him seriously. "No, Logan. Everything is not ok! Just look at this place. What used to be so peaceful and happy, turned into something violent and chaotic. Imagine all the animals and people a—and the little kids. And on top of all that, we're stuck in a fire ring that keeps on growing every second and is going to kill us. Face it Logan. We're done. We couldn't save any of them and we can't save ourselves." Tears sped down her cheek. She couldn't control it anymore. But Logan was quiet, staring at the rising flames. He took a deep breath. Holly glanced at him and was surprised to see tears rolling down his cheek as well.

Holly stood up, about to comfort him, when Logan looked at her straight in the eye, his ocean blue eyes glittering. "Holly, this is probably the last time I can ever talk to you again. But I really, really need to know something. Why did you stop hanging out with me all of a sudden? I thought we were best friends, but w—what happened?" He looked genuinely sad.

This was the question she had been avoiding all this time. But now she didn't really have a choice, but to give a straight answer.

Holly sighed. "Well, remember when the sports tournaments were happening in sixth grade and you shot a basketball from the other side of the court?" Logan nodded. "And people were so impressed and started calling you the basketball king and all? I wasn't jealous or anything, but then you started hanging out with them. At first I didn't really mind, but then you started ignoring me. Like…completely ignoring me. And so, I thought that you left me because of your popularity." A look of realization shone upon Logan's face. He slapped his forehead. "Oh my goodness, Holly. I'm so sorry, but that's a misunderstanding. I never wanted to actually hang out with them. They were kind of pushing me to hang out, you know? A lot of them were asking me questions about the shot and all that. Some of them even wanted me to give them lessons. I mean, I didn't want to be rude so I kind of went along with them."

Holly's eyes widened. "What? Why didn't you tell me this?"

Logan swept his hand through his chestnut brown hair. "Actually Holly, I've tried talking to you a lot of times. You—you didn't really give me a chance to explain." Suddenly it hit Holly. All this time, she had blamed Logan for being a bad friend, when it was really her that was the bad friend. Whenever Logan had tried talking to her in the halls or anywhere else, she avoided him. It was all because of the thought that *he* was the one who left, *he* was the bad friend, which had been pasted inside her brain all these years. She was so ashamed of herself.

"Logan! I'm such an idiot. All this time, I blamed everything on you! I—I—I am so sorry." She sobbed. Logan shook his head. "Holly, don't cry. It wasn't completely your fault, I mean I should have been a bit more—" "No Logan! Don't blame it all on yourself. It's my fault. It's all my fault!" She had never in her life cried like this before. She leaned against the surprisingly smooth bark, and looked at Logan, who looked guilty. "Don't look so guilty Logan. You did nothing wrong." She looked at the flames moving faster every second and sniffed. "I guess the thought of you not wanting to be my best friend anymore really brought me to overthink. Really though, deep inside I was more sad then mad. I just acted tough around you to make you think I was doing just fine."

Tears began rolling down Logan's face again. "Hey did I make you cry, Logan? I thought you weren't a crier. What happened now?" She tried. She felt hot, because the fire was really close to them, just inches away. Logan wiped his eyes. "Well, I guess this is good bye." He said motioning towards the flames. "But before anything," His voice cracked as he continued. "Can we go back to being best—"

He didn't need to continue. Holly nodded as she felt the heat of the fire near her face. "Yes!" she said loudly. "No matter what happens, we'll always be best friends. No more misunderstandings!" Logan cried tears of joy as he held his arms out. Holly gave him a big hug. This would be it. But she was glad Logan was by her side. Holly took in the scent of Logan's favourite cologne, hoping this would be the last scent that she remembered, so she remembered him, the greatest friend anyone could ask for, forever…

Holly suddenly didn't feel hot anymore. She couldn't feel the heat of the fire either. *Am I dead? No that can't be right, I still feel Logan and smell his cologne.* She was about to pull away from Logan, when she felt something, a light shining towards her. "Logan do you feel—" she stopped. The fire ring around them was gone completely. Not a trace left of it. Logan looked around confused. "Woah, I thought we were going to get eaten up by the fire ring. What happened?" He had just finished talking, when something shone towards them. They looked in its direction and gasped. It just so happened that the wolves had thrown them under the willow tree with the plaque. They hadn't caught sight of plaque, and just threw them towards the nearest tree.

Holly shook her head. "Oh no, everyone forgot about the plaque during all this chaos. And we didn't notice because of our waterworks." She looked closer. The plaque was burnt out and cracked, but the heart square was slowly shining, dimly at first but increasing in brightness. The cracks around the square were starting to mend.

Holly pulled the plaque from tree. "I thought that the plaque would completely be ruined after the wolves came, but what happened to that one square?" Logan examined it. Holly thought hard, about the history of the plaque, Luna's vision, the wolves. She walked slowly to the other side of the willow tree, grasping the plaque. Logan followed quietly.

For the first time since all the turmoil, Holly wasn't scared or nervous. She felt strong and determined. She looked at the plaque, burnt out with only one shining square. Then she looked at Crystal Clearing.

Although the situation wasn't getting any better, Holly observed something she hadn't noticed since the start of the wolf attack.

In a corner, Chuck was pulling Ophelia away from a wolf who was biting and clawing at her, all while other wolves were hurting him. "Chuck! Go save yourself! Your getting hurt!" The frightened unicorn cried. "No!" Chuck grunted, pulling with all his might, while one wolf dug his claws into the bear's fur.

Not far from them, Kelly was bandaging up a man's arm covered in blood, holding Jessi close. A large stone whacked her in the face causing her to groan in pain. But she still prioritized the man's hand. Jessi gave his sister a hug, sobbing.

Under a tree, an old lady sat with crying children huddled around her, trying to comfort them.

A bit further back, a young child sat on the ground crying, while a wolf was sneakily coming up behind him, about to pounce. Seeing this, a lion jumped in front of the wolf to protect the child, only to have the wolf bite him.

Holly realized that the inhabitants of Crystal Clearing were trying to protect others more then themselves. She looked down at the plaque, which was starting to glow dimly. Luna's vision suddenly popped up in her head. "Yellow roses. Lotus flowers." She murmured. "Holly, what are you doing?" Logan asked. Holly looked up. "Lotus flowers! Yellow roses!" She repeated. She looked at Logan. "Oh my goodness, I understand Luna's vision! How did we not see this from the start?" She felt so happy.

"Luna's vision? What about it?" Logan asked confused. Holly smiled. "Remember her vision starts out with the Clearing on fire, and then a yellow rose and a lotus flower fall on it? Well, yellow roses represent friendship and

Lotus flowers are symbols of compassion and peace. Haven't you noticed that all this time, the people and animals are prioritizing other's safety more then theirs? That's their compassion and friendship towards others. That's their biggest power!" Logan's eyes widened. "You're right! And I think the reason the heart square started glowing was because we broke our misunderstanding and grudge right in front of it!" Holly nodded. "That would totally make sense!" She looked down at the plaque. It was glowing dimly.

Logan looked determined. "We have to bring the plaque closer to all these acts of compassion. I think it senses them." Holly pointed to a tree near Ophelia and Chuck. "Quick! Let's run to that tree!" Holly and Logan managed to run to the tree without drawing much attention to themselves. Chuck was still trying to save Ophelia, while Ophelia was trying to tell Chuck to save himself. Everyone was too distracted to notice Holly pointing the plaque in their direction. The animal square started brightening up.

But the wolves howled letting Chuck and Ophelia go. They made a whole bunch of growling noises and ran off. "Great! Two squares down, two more to go!" Holly says, facing Logan. Then the human square started glowing.

Sure enough, Kelly had approached Ophelia and Chuck and was bandaging and helping them up. Holly grinned. "Make that one more square to go!" Logan motioned towards them. "Let's go tell them and see if they are ok." Ophelia and Chuck looked dazed but Ophelia caught sight of Logan and Holly jogging their way. "Holly! Logan! Are you guys ok? Where have you two been all this time? And…is that the plaque? Oh no we completely forgot about the plaque!" She gasped. Chuck looked at it closely. "Wait, is it… glowing?" Holly was about to answer when they heard a deep voice scream, "you! You two ruin everything!"

They all looked to see Alister walking towards them angrily. Holly noticed that the crystal he wore around his neck had a small crack. "First you two inform everyone we're coming, then you try and mess with my wolves." The two wolves that had ran away from Ophelia and Chuck were behind Alister, twitching and grunting. Alister touched his crystal firmly and they instantly stopped grunting and twitching and looked ready to pounce. Logan frowned. "Did you see that? He's controlling all the wolves! I bet they were normal wolves until he started wearing that crystal." He whispered.

Alister howled and then a wolf pounced on Holly from behind, causing her to send the plaque flying towards Alister, who was moving towards it with speed. "No!!" She screamed. But Logan sprinted towards it, jumped up in the air, and expertly caught it like a basketball. Holly wiggled around, trying to free herself from the wolf. Thankfully, the animal wasn't hurting or paining her now. Then she noted that the wolf's eyes were dull and stationary. They didn't move at all and seemed kind of like they were dead inside. Logan's statement about the wolves being brainwashed by Alister using that crystal made sense now.

Alister howled again, furious. Logan held the plaque tightly. "It's over, Alister!" Logan announced. He sounded brave and heroic, but Holly could see he was shaking. She wrestled harder, wishing she could help him. "This isn't over!" The old wolf screamed. "I will get that plaque, destroy it and rule!" Logan shook his head. "No you won't, Alister! Don't you see? This plaque runs on compassion and friendship.

While those two things are still among the people of Crystal Clearing, you will never be able to destroy it." Holly stopped squirming around and listened. She had never heard Logan speak so powerfully.

Logan's eyes narrowed. "Their compassion is so strong, that your little crystal won't help you brainwash them." Alister growled. "How dare you speak about me like that!" He shot the electric blue lightning from his eyes. Holly wanted to jump out and push him to the side, yet she couldn't. But Logan pulled the plaque in front of him as a shield. To everyone's surprise, the plaque shone as bright as sunlight. Alister tried pushing with all his might, but the plaque was stronger.

Holly marvelled at the sight. She had only seen things like this in movies. It was a battle of magic, one side golden light, the other electric blue lightning. Some village folk ran to help Logan hold the plaque. Holly looked over at her captor wolf. He wasn't pinning her down fully, but looked every irritated. He was making weird noises and was shaking his head vigorously. Before Holly could do anything, the plaque shone brighter than ever. A whole sky of light erupted and for a few moments no one could see anything.

But the blanket of light slowly faded away revealing Crystal Clearing, more beautiful than before. Bright green trees stood tall and proud. Butterflies fluttered through the air, happily. A dazzling rainbow arched over the place. And in the distance, the majestic waterfall flowed swiftly and calmly.

Holly rubbed her eyes and tried to sit up, but felt a great weight on her back. "Ouch!" She muttered, dropping down. Then she heard a groan. Then another one. Followed by an "oh, wha—what happened?" The weight on her back moved and she saw the wolf standing near her, yawning and rubbing his eyes. He caught sight of Holly mid yawn. He looked disoriented. "Uhh, who are you?" He looked around. "Where am I? Why do I feel like I've been sleeping for ages?" He frowned. "And was I lying on top of you?" He gasped. "What is going on?"

Holly sat up and rolled her eyes. "Firstly, my name is Holly Mitchell. Nice to meet you! Second, your in a magical place called Crystal Clearing. Thirdly, you haven't been sleeping, you've been brainwashed by your," Holly snorted.

"Alpha leader." She examined her arms, which were full of cuts and bite marks. "And lastly... why don't you take a good look at these?" She stretched her arms out in front of him. The wolf looked confused as he stared from Holly to the bite marks. He blinked. "Why are you showing me your scratches? Wait, I didn't do that did I?" Holly sighed. "Umm, yeah you totally did. Why else do you think I'm showing you my arm? To be exact actually, you were trying to pin me down. These happened because I was wrestling out of your grasp, so technically they're my fault. But don't get me wrong, you were totally the villain." The wolf looked irritated but at the same time slightly amused. "Ok first of all, I would never do that! Who do you think I am, some kind of psycho wolf? Listen kid, you're obviously very imaginative, but please don't portray me of all people as some kind of psycho." He shakes, disgusted. Holly crossed her arms. "Oh if you're so disgusted by psycho wolf then how do you explain—" she stops. She was expecting to see the wrecked Clearing, but instead found herself astonished by the new beauty of the Clearing. The place seemed more brighter and magical than before. "What? Explain what? Kid, you ok?"

The wolf nagged. Holly lost interest in him and looked around at the dazed people and animals, slowly getting up. "Woah, what is everyone doing here?" The wolf came from behind Holly and moved towards a wolf that was sitting up looking like he was going to throw up. "Atlas? What happened to you, bud?" He went over and started talking to him.

Holly went over to Logan, who was rubbing his head. The plaque lay on his lap. "Holly!" He says, standing up. "Hey, that was some sick dialogue you shot at Alister. I've never seen you so heroic before." Holly said, giving her friend a pat on the back. Logan smirked. "Awe, are you jealous, Holly?" He joked. Holly shook her head. "Instead of a pat I should have given you a smack." She pretended to be annoyed.

"Holly! Logan!" A bubbly voice called. They turned and saw Ophelia and Chuck making their way towards them, followed by Jessi. He ran straight into Logan's outstretched arms. "Logan! You're a hero!" He looked over at Holly. "You too, Holly! You both are heroes." Logan shrugged. "Oh, I wouldn't call us heroes or anything. We're Just, you know, your friends." Holly nodded. "Your best friends, who want to see you happy." Jessi clapped. "You guys are my heroes and best friends!" Chuck gave them both high fives. "Great job, guys!" He said, proudly. Ophelia's emerald green eyes sparkled with admiration. "Wow! I can't believe you guys saved the Clearing! The Crystal flies were right after all!" She looked like she was going to burst.

Mention of the Crystal flies made Holly think about what had happened at the cave. She gasped. "The Crystal flies!" She exclaimed. "They were completely correct! Remember at the cave, they flew to me and Logan, and then to the rocks and then to you, Ophelia?" The unicorn nodded. "I think they meant me and Logan had to come together, and go back to being friends, just like you and Chuck. Remember after they fluttered around us, they moved some rocks that were sitting apart from each other closer? Then they flew to you and near the cave entrance, possibly referring to Chuck, pointing out your friendship!" Logan smiled. "I'm telling you, this girl has a secret talent for understanding riddles." Ophelia and Chuck beamed at each other. "That would totally make sense! But, um I thought you guys were already friends." Holly slapped her forehead. "Turns out, I also have a talent for blurting things out." Logan grinned. "That's a long story filled with misunderstandings, tears and even more tears. We'll tell you later." "Awe! Don't keep us in suspense! Tell us, please! We all thought you two were best friends!" Ophelia pleaded. Everyone laughed. "We shouldn't have underestimated the Crystal flies, though." Holly says.

Suddenly the Crystal flies flew towards them. They flittered around in a sort of "we told you so" kinda way. Ophelia looks at them. "We're sorry for underestimating you beautiful flies." She says apologetically. They swirled around in an "apology accepted" way. They giggled as the magnificent flies flew away.

"Ah, there you kids are. I've been looking for you!" Said a voice from behind them. They turned and saw Luna walking towards them. "Luna! Are you ok? We—we thought you..." Chuck's voice trailed off. The old wolf laughed. "Oh no no, I was just weak, because I haven't used my powers in a while. Kelly was going around treating everyone, so she took care of my scars and scratches." Ophelia jumped around. "You didn't tell us you had powers! It was sooo cool! It was a battle of electric lightning. I was totally freaked out, but when I saw that, the freak out went POOF! But then it was back when, you know, the wolves started attacking." The little unicorn shivered at the thought.

Luna's face darkened. "I knew those wolves. Most of them were very powerful, but wanted to use their powers for good. But you see Alister, had no powers and was envious of the more powerful ones. I had the chance to talk with a good friend of mine, Azure. He was the nicest and most powerful wolf there. But from what he tells me, Alister grew more envious and spent hours doing dark magic. He produced a crystal that he used to not only brainwash all the powerful wolves, but also take their powers. He wanted to rule and spread negativity everywhere." She sighed. "I was one of the powerful wolves, but I never showed anyone, because my parent urged me not to. I think they were growing suspicious of Alister. Then my father went to confront him, and…you know the rest." She closed her eyes.

"The way he controlled the wolves was really creepy. They were so strong! And trust me I've seen many strong people in my life. But no one as strong as those wolves!" Logan remarked. Luna nodded.

Holly looked around, concerned. "Hey speaking of Alister, where is he? And his necklace, too." Luna stood tall. "Ah, don't worry about that, Holly. I've got it covered." Just as she finished, a shout could be heard coming from behind a tree. A tall, slender man and a lion emerged carrying Alister and Clementine. Another wolf followed them. They made their way towards Luna, while the wolf kicked and shouted. "Let me go, you jerks. You don't know who you are messing with. I'm Alister the—" "yeah yeah, Alister the Alpha who will control the world. You said that several times already." Says the tall guy.

Alister growled when he saw Luna. "Oh, what are you still doing here alive? I thought I already made away with you." Luna looked at her paws. "Yes, yes that's what you thought. But unfortunately for you, I am one of the powerful wolves." Alister screamed. "Betrayer! If I had your power, I would have ruled the world by now! How did I not notice! Grr." He frowned. "Oh I see, it was because of those creatures you call your parents. Those jerks." He squirmed around trying to pounce, but failed. Clementine was back to her human self, a little old lady with torn clothes. She just looked dazed and didn't say a word.

The wolf behind them, who Holly recognized as the one she had talked with earlier, came forward. "Alister stop trying. Don't you see that you're practically nothing without your little crystal?" Ophelia sniffed. "Yeah, you both should try and experience what we experienced when your brainwashed wolves pinned us to the ground. We were unable to move, we tried with all our might, but no luck." She say dramatically. Alister wiggled even harder. He caught sight of Holly and Logan. "You! This is all because of you. One day I will find you and tear your souls!" He hollered. Luna rolled her eyes. "Please take them to my cave. There's a cage at the back, put them both in there." She asked the man and lion, who nodded and started walking away, with Alister shouting and squirming.

She turned to the other wolf. "And Azure I assume you have the crystal?" Azure nodded and showed them the crystal. Ophelia backed up. Azure laughed. "Don't worry, this thing is pretty useless now. Anyone want to keep it as jewelry?" Ophelia gasped. "And relive the horrendous memories? Never ever!" She shrieked. Azure smiled. "It's ok, I understand. If no one wants it

I'll just destroy it myself." He threw it down and crushed it with his paw.

Then he cleared his throat. "Alright! Now that that's over, let's move on to apologizes." He looked guilty and embarrassed, as he moved towards Holly. "Um, hi. We've met earlier. I'm Azure." Holly crossed her arms. "Oh yeah, I remember." She examined her hands. Azure giggled nervously. "Yeah, right, of course. Um, so you were right. Those bite marks are totally mine. And I wanted to apologize because as you probably know, I was brainwashed by Alister and I had absolutely no idea what I was doing. And I really need you to know that I would never ever bite or pin down anyone! So... I'm sorry." He looked really uncomfortable. Holly looked over at Logan, Ophelia, Chuck and Luna, who all had amused expressions on their faces. Holly leaned over to Azure. "You better be thankful that I've been hanging out with these good folks for the last couple days. If I was my old self, I would've given you a nice punch or two." She whispered, jokingly. Azure smiled awkwardly. "So...we're good?" He asked. Holly grinned. "We're good." She said putting out her fist for a bump. Azure looked relived and bumped his paw on her fist. He then went over to Ophelia and Chuck. "And I owe an apology to you two." He looked at Chuck's furry leg, which had a big white bandaid. "Gosh, how's your leg?" Azure asked sadly. Chuck smiled. "It's all good. I'm just happy that everything is back to normal and that no one's controlling you." Ophelia nodded. "Yeah! I thought you were all just a bunch of psycho wolves who love violence more than anything. But it's good to know that you all are really nice and willing to apologize." Azure tried smiling. "So, we're good?" Ophelia and Chuck grinned. "Yup! We're all good!" They said together. Azure exhaled. "Oh good. Two apologies down. Many more to go."

Just then another wolf came their way. "Hey you, kid." He said gesturing at Logan. "If I remember correctly, I had pulled you across the ground to a tree and banged you into it. So as apology I'm giving you a rock that you may throw at me, to cool your fury towards me." He said, handing Logan a rock and standing in front of him. "I apologized to the other people and surprisingly they didn't throw the rock. You're the last person." He shrugged nonchalantly. Logan picked up the rock, took a deep breath…

and threw it behind him into a lake. The wolf watched. "Do you know why The other people didn't throw The rock at you? Because that's their power of forgiveness. Now I'm an outsider, but if there's anything I've learned from being in Crystal Clearing and meeting all the people that live here, it's that compassion, forgiveness and friendship are the things that really matter. So I'm not going to throw anything at you. Let's hug it out shall we?" He went over to the grateful wolf and gave him a big hug. The wolf smiled. "Yeah, you guys are all amazing."

Suddenly A look of confusion filled Azure's face. "Wait a minute, I realized something. Where are we going to live now? When Alister was controlling us, he just had us all travel and stay at the nearest place, like nomads. But what about now?" Luna smiled graciously. "Why look any further, Azure? You can stay with us in Crystal Clearing!" Azure and the other wolf looked at each other. "Really? After all we've done to you, you're willing to accept us into your home?" He asked, taken aback. At that moment, all the villagers were starting to gather around them, hearing the conversation. Chuck nodded. "You heard what Logan said. Our compassion and friendship towards each other is what saved our Clearing. Sure you weren't very nice to us in the beginning, but you were brainwashed. So it isn't your fault." He says, kindly. Luna puts a paw on Azure's back. "He's right, Azure. They welcomed me years ago when I was without a place to go. And now we're ready to welcome you." Ophelia smiled so widely, that you could see all her teeth. "Yeah, we're ready to give you all a second chance!" She exclaimed. "Welcome to your new home!" Everyone cheered. Holly and Logan stood watching the happy creatures. Ophelia was jumping around all the wolves. Chuck was shaking one's paw. Luna was happily talking to Azure. Jessi seemed to have made a new wolf friend.

"I'm so glad that the Clearing is back to its happy, magical self." Holly commented, feeling so proud. "Yeah, me too. And I'm also glad that we're best friends again." Logan said, grinning. Holly put her arm on his shoulder and beamed. Logan looked at the sky.

"Hey I've been meaning to ask you something. How did you know all that stuff about flowers? You never struck me as the type to be interested in that kind of thing." Holly nodded. "You're right, I'm not. I learned it from Latisha. You know her total tomboy yet soft girly girl personality. I'm telling you that girl knows everything about flowers. And by everything, I mean everything." Logan whistled. "Wow, Latisha! I almost forgot all about her. Oh now that everything's good, I can't wait to talk to her again." He smiled. Holly sighed. "And I can't wait for Latisha's "I told you you should just talk with Logan" dialogue when I get back home." Logan laughed.

Just then, Luna called for everyone's attention. "Alright, now that that is settled, we can't forget about the two wonderful kids who played a part in saving our Clearing, now can we?" She turned to Holly and Logan, motioning for them to come closer. They looked at each other and started walking. Everyone's eyes were on them as they moved forward. Holly felt herself turning red. She'd never in her life been shy before, but now she felt nervous having all these people watch her. Luna smiled proudly at them. "If it weren't for you two, we might not be standing here now. You two were guests, but after all the things you done, I am honoured to say that you both are a part of this big family." Holly was so touched. "You shouldn't be thanking us, we should be thanking you all. After seeing your affection towards each other and to us newcomers, I honestly feel like I've changed a lot. And if it weren't for you, I would always have a misunderstanding pressed deep into my heart." She glanced at Logan, who looked like he was holding back tears. Luna turned to Chuck, who came holding the plaque. "As thanks, we want you both to put the newly repaired plaque back into the Willow tree." Holly and Logan couldn't be happier. "We would be honoured!" They replied in unison. They took the plaque, Holly holding one side while Logan held the other side, and slowly started their way to the Willow tree. Along the way, they saw Chuck smiling and Ophelia blinking back tears. Kelly was holding Jessi, who gave them a thumbs up. Every person and animal there looked so proud and happy. Even some wolves gave them grateful grins. They reached the tree and with a deep breath they pushed the plaque towards the tree. A blinding light shone from it and there it was engraved into the tree. Everyone cheered joyfully. Jessi ran and gave them a big hug. Ophelia, Chuck, Kelly, Luna, and all the village folk congratulated them and gave them hugs, high fives and fist bumps.

Ophelia cleared her throat. "Ahem. Um, If I remember correctly, you have a story to tell us." She batted her eyelashes. Holly's eyes widened. "Seriously? You still remember that?" Ophelia nodded innocently. Logan shook his head. "You're not gonna leave us alone until we explain, are you?" Ophelia grinned. He sighed. "Alright everyone gather around, it's story time!" Some Village folk stood there eagerly. "And you might want to sit down, it's going to be long." Holly added. Everyone laughed…

Holly and Logan were invited to spend the next 2 days in Crystal Clearing.

After the story (which had Ophelia crying) everyone was busy welcoming the wolves and Ophelia was the one who gave them a grand tour of the Clearing. A lady from the Clearing named Bianca, who seemed to be the village dressmaker, offered to sew any rips on Holly and Logan's clothing. After, Logan had gone out with Jessi and Holly returned to Kelly's hut to check her phone, which she had completely forgotten about. She was bewildered by the 20 texts from Latisha and her parents. She replied to them all, but didn't tell anyone about the Clearing.

In the evening there was a party! Food, games, sports, and lots of laughter. Holly had so much fun! The next day, the party continued, along with the fun.

Before she knew it, it was time to go back. She and Logan were met at the entrance by all the people, animals and wolves. Logan was giving Jessi a big hug. "Awe man, I'm going to miss you, little guy." He says. He then rummages around in his bag and pulls out a keychain with a basketball. He hands it to Jessi. "Here's a little something so you never forget me." Jessi grabs it eagerly. "Wow. I'll never forget you, Logan!" He gives him one last hug, and moved towards Holly. "I'll never forget you too, Holly!" Holly gives him a big hug. "You know, I wish I had you as my little brother. It would have been awesome!" She rummages around her own duffle bag and pulls out a similar keychain with a soccer ball. It was her absolute favourite keychain. "Here. Take this too." She says. Jessi jumps up and down. "Wow, two presents? You guys are the best!" Kelly comes up next with a few fruits in a small basket. "For your travel back." She says, handing it to Holly. "Thank you for being the best visitors we've ever had!" Holly smiled. "And thank you for making me feel all better after my, you know, pass out." She blushed. "It was my pleasure." Kelly insists. Ophelia and Chuck are up next. "Awe, I don't want you guys to leave!" Ophelia pouts. Logan laughs. "We don't want to leave either Ophelia. We're just leaving because we absolutely have to. If we didn't, we totally wouldn't be leaving anytime soon." Holly sighed. "I'm gonna miss your bubbly voice, Ophelia." She says, giving her a hug. Logan did so too. "Have a nice trip. I hope you get to where you need, safely." Chuck chimes in, holding his arms out. Holly and Logan sink into Chuck's warm embrace. Logan gestures to Ophelia and Chuck. "Stay best friends, ok? Never let misunderstandings ruin your friendship!" He says, as the unicorn and bear beam brightly. Luna came last and bowed her head. "Once again I thank you for helping protect our Clearing. You are welcome to come here anytime you want. But unfortunately I must ask you to keep our Clearing a secret. If anyone else find out, you never know what will happen. Some, obviously are good hearted kids like you. But there are people out there with a bad heart." Logan nodded. "We understand. As much as we want to tell everyone about Crystal Clearing, we'll make sure to keep it a secret." Luna smiles. "Thank you for understanding."

Holly didn't want to leave this beautiful place. She wanted to stay here with all these amazing people and animals. Then, she had an idea. "Wait! Before we go, do you guys mind if I take a picture of all of us together? That way, I'll never forget any of you!" Everyone agreed and got together. Holly raised her phone and clicked.

There it was, the perfect picture. Logan standing happily beside Kelly, who was holding a smiling Jessi. Ophelia was grinning so wildly while Chuck, all smiles, was giving a thumbs up. Luna stood by the side, beaming regally. Along the back the beautiful scenery was stunning. Holly smiled satisfied.

"When can we see you again?" Ophelia asks, teary eyed. Holly and Logan looked at each other. "We're not sure exactly when, but…soon." Holly assures her.

The crystal flies led them out of the Clearing. Luna had arranged for the Crystal flies to show the way back. With one last wave to all the inhabitants of Crystal Clearing, they were off. They hadn't walked far when the Crystal flies stopped in front of a large, bushy plant. Behind it was the campground. "Thank you Crystal flies for all your help!" Holly exclaimed, as the flies flew back. Holly started walking in, but Logan stopped her. "Wait! Let's check the time first." He pulled out his phone. "9:00 sharp. Oh no, we don't know anything that's going on at camp! What if we get caught or someone noticed we were gone?" He remarked. Holly took a deep breath. "Well, we're just going to have to face it. C'mon." She pulled him along, trying not to be noticeable.

Some kids were sitting on camp chairs talking, reading, taking a nap. It looked like free time. "Campers?" Called a voice behind them. They turned to see Linda standing there arms crossed. She frowned. "Wait a minute, you two weren't with us yesterday, or actually the..." Her voice trailed off. She scrunched up her nose, closed her eyes and shook her head. When she opened them, she looked around the campground and then at them. "Hey, did you two need something?" She asked, eyebrows raised. "Um, yeah we were actually looking for you. Um, we, I mean I needed a bandaid. Nothing happened, just a little cut." Logan stammered. Linda looked at their bags. "Um, we were rummaging around in our bags for one, but couldn't find any." Holly says quickly. "Alright, follow me." She said leading them to a tent. She disappeared inside, and then appeared with a couple bandaids. "You want me to take a look at the cut?" She asked. "No, no it's fine. I just scratched my arm really badly. Nothing else." He says, pretending to pick a bandaid. Linda shrugged. "Ok then, have a good break, you two." "Break?" Holly blurted out. Linda raised one eyebrow suspiciously. "Yeah, break. Aren't you guys tired from all those activities and challenges that we did yesterday? Your councillor told you about the extra long break, didn't they?" She questioned. "Oh, no she did. It's just, um, you know we're not really tired or anything, so um yeah." Logan mentioned quickly. Linda put her arms on her hips. "Not tired? Wow, that's a first. Usually everyone's exhausted after those intense activities. Pretty impressive, I must say." She says. Holly and Logan smiled. "We both play sports a lot." Holly replied. Linda grinned. "Ah, I see! Well, even if you guys aren't tired, just rest up K? We're doing some more today." And with that she walked into the tent. Holly and Logan sighed in relief. "Phew! We managed to get away with that. And I got free bandaids!" Logan says putting them into his bag. Holly grins. "Can you believe that they don't remember anything? Wow, must be some magic from Crystal Clearing." Logan nodded as he finishes zipping up his backpack. "I mean, we weren't technically lying about anything. We totally were doing some intense activities a couple days ago." Holly laughs…

After spending one more day at the campground, the group returned to the cabins. They had a big party since it was the last full day. It was fun, but nothing compared to the Crystal Clearing celebrations.

Then it was Wednesday, the day they would be leaving. Tammy said a few words of thanks and how to sign up for summer camp. They did all their chores, played some games, and before they knew it, it was time to leave.

Holly and Logan made their way outside. "So, are you gonna sign up for summer camp?" Holly asked as they waited for their parents. Logan nodded. "Oh yeah, definitely! Believe it or not, I never wanted to go to camp, but my parents forced me to go." Holly gasped. "Oh my gosh, same! I was so not looking forward to coming, but after everything that happened, I'm definitely signing up for summer camp." Logan chuckled. "And of course by 'signing up for camp' you actually mean visiting Crystal Clearing!" Holly winked. "Exactly!"

Just then, a blue pickup Truck rolled its way into the parking lot. "That's my ride!" Logan says. The window rolls down to reveal Logan's mom, wearing glittery pink sunglasses. She had chestnut brown hair, which cascaded down her shoulder in soft curls and she had on her signature bright red lipstick. Holly had never seen Logan's mom without it. She remembered Mrs. Fitzgerald as sweet and bubbly, sort of like Ophelia, from all the times she had been to Logan's house. She was a Hairstylist and owned her own salon, which she ran with her sister. Holly had been there before, and the service was awesome.

"Hi Mrs. Fitzgerald!" Holly called, waving. "Oh hello there, love! I haven't seen you in a while." She said, in her Australian accent. Logan opened the doors and climbed in. "You want a ride Holly? There's plenty of space at the back." Mrs Fitzgerald offered. Holly shook her head. "Thanks Mrs. Fitzgerald, but my parents will be here soon!" "Alright, g'day, love." She says waving. Logan waved from inside the car. Just a couple minutes after the truck had pulled out, her parents' Minivan came in. Her parents came out and greeted her with hugs. "Wow, is that a smile I see on your face?" Her mom asks. "Seems like someone enjoyed nature camp." Her dad calls from the driver's seat. Holly climbed into the back to find Hendrick playing a video game on his iPad. "Hi Holly." He says, still focusing on his game. Holly noticed he was still wearing her baseball cap. "You know, nature camp wasn't so bad. I'm thinking of going in summer." She says casually as she pulls the door shut. Her parents gasped and Hendrick looked up from his game. "See, I told you you were going to love it. You loved it so much that you want to go next year! Yay!" Her mom eagerly claps her hands. Hendrick snorted. "Oh really? What about your King of Lights show? I heard some people at camp say there was a movie coming up in summer." Holly shrugged. "It's fine. I'll just stream it another time. Camping was a new experience that I really liked." She said. It was true. The adventure she had in Crystal Clearing was way better than any sci-fi movie. And the actual camp wasn't so bad either. Her dad pulled out of the parking lot and onto the road. "Oh yeah, guess what? Logan was at that camp too!" Holly says. Her mom smiled.

"Oh, I see why you're so happy." She turned to Holly eagerly. "So, tell me everything that happened." Holly grinned. She couldn't have asked for a better Spring holiday...

TWO WEEKS LATER

Holly, Logan and Latisha were at Holly's house streaming "The King Of Lights." When It was commercial break, Latisha leaned back. "You know, I never thought I'd see us all sitting here doing something we loved, after your guys' little grudge." She says, taking a sip of soda. "Yeah, same! I thought we were done. Like completely done!" Logan said, grabbing a pack of chips. Holly picked up her phone and clicked on photos. She would look at the Crystal Clearing picture almost every day, wondering what Ophelia would be chattering about, what Jessi was doing with his keychains, how the new wolves were settling in, what Chuck and Kelly were doing. She sighed remembering the wonderful memories. She was propping her legs up onto the couch, when she accidentally dropped her phone. It fell right where Latisha's feet were. Holly tried to grab it fast, but Latisha pick it up first. "Woah, careful Holly." She laughs reaching to give it back, when something catches her eyes. On the screen was the picture from Crystal Clearing! She frowned, looking closer at it. Holly tried grabbing the phone from her. "Uh, Latisha? Can I have my phone back? Please? Come on Latisha." But Latisha was looking at the picture, horrified. "OMG! Is that a unicorn? And...a bear?!" She yelped. Latisha was super afraid of bears. "Oh, but that was the nicest bear ever, Lati." Logan said, only to have Holly poke him in the ribs. "Um, it's, it's just photoshop, Latisha. We took a picture at camp and edited ourselves into that picture." She tried, glaring at Logan, who mouthed 'sorry.'

Latisha put the phone down and looked at Holly and Logan doubtfully. "Holly, Logan, what *really* happened at that camp?" She questioned, like an interrogation officer. "Nothing happened, Lati. It's all good." Holly quickly mentioned. Latisha leaned forward. "Oh don't you lie to me, Holly. I know you two are hiding something that happened at Camp Green Vine." She said, arms crossed. Holly glanced at Logan. There was no way they could hide anything from Latisha.

The girl was like a mini detective. She sighed, taking back her phone. "Ok, fine. We'll tell you." Logan clasped his hands in front of him. "Oh and Latisha, you might want to sit down. It's a long story." He added. Latisha looked at them confused. Holly and Logan eyed one another, and took a deep breath. "So, Latisha." Holly began, smiling mischievously. "Do you believe in magic?"

The End

CPSIA information can be obtained
at www.ICGtesting.com
Printed in the USA
LVHW050020210123
737602LV00004B/222